ALSO BY ANNE RENWICK

ELEMENTAL WEB TALES

A
SNOWFLAKE
AT
MIDNIGHT

ANNE RENWICK

USA TODAY BESTSELLING AUTHOR

A Snowflake at Midnight/ Anne Renwick. — 1st ed.

ISBN 978-1-948359-55-9

Cover design by Aaricia from Malice and Mayhem Book Covers.

Edited by Sandra Sookoo.

To all librarians, past, present and future.

Thank you to...

The modern medievalists studying ancient medical texts. Your hunt for past remedies that might be brought into our present inspired the idea for this book.

The British Library and all those associated individuals who made it possible for me to flip the virtual pages of rare manuscripts from my very own desk.

The biomedical researchers who published papers on *viscum album* detailing the many properties it possesses.

The Plotmonkeys—Kristan Higgins, Joss Day, Jennifer Iszkiewicz, Stacia Bjarnason and Huntley Fitzpatrick. A special thanks to Joss for - once again - letting me toss ideas at her through the internet.

Sandra Sookoo, my wonderful editor who mercilessly ferrets out weaknesses and sets my work on a better course.

My readers, your enthusiasm makes all the difference.

My husband and all the conversations that went into the making of this story.

My mom and dad who taught me to love reading at an early age.

Mr. Fox, the English teacher who lived next door. I'll never forget all the wonderful books he placed in my hands or the way he wielded his red pen without mercy upon my earliest works. "Scrap this and try again" was a hard lesson, but one worth learning.

CHAPTER ONE

London
December 24, 1884

"Y ou look quite fetching, Miss Brown. Festive yet decorous." Dr. Bracken leaned over the sturdy circulation desk that separated them and propped his chin on his hand. "I approve." Bright eyes underscored by a curling mustache and an amused smile gazed up at her, waiting. But they'd long since lost their charm.

Irritation prickled. Most patrons were respectful of her position, but not all. She'd learned it was best not to respond to such personal observations, lest she find herself steered into a quagmire. Before her idled the greatest repeat offender. Her grip tightened upon the rubber stamp in her hand. Hurling it was, alas, not an option. "Is there something the library can provide for you, Dr. Bracken?"

An hour past, warm air had stopped rising from the heating grates. A gentle prodding to empty the halls of the Lister Institute. Though the building would be officially closed for the holidays, its scientists, who all but resided within its walls, required the reminder to set aside their pipettes and flasks, to shut down their aetheric microscopes, to spend time with their family members.

Alas, one particular chemist was in no hurry to leave.

She eyed the crisp knot of his cravat, a clear cry for attention. Unusual at this late hour in the day. Who kept a supply of such starched items in a research laboratory? A man with a need to impress. And, for the moment, one convinced of her appreciation.

"It always provides the most lovely view." His words oozed, sticky and sweet. "But, of course, I've come to see what brilliant, new ideas you have for me today."

Evie stamped another book as she bit back bitter remarks and swallowed, leaving them churning in her stomach. Her next words were clipped. "I'm a research librarian, not a scientist."

Though she was also a trained medievalist, such was her current title. All personal scholarship took place after hours, tucked into tiny spaces between other obligations.

Of late, too much pulled her in too many directions. Work. Papa. A certain attractive young man from the botany department. A man who was—she snuck a glance at the clock—overdue. Mr. Lockwood was one particular diversion that she did not mind in the least, even if escalating flirtations left her in a continuous state of frustration. But it was their decision to speak with Mr. Davies, head librarian, about their joint project this evening that kept nervous dragonflies zipping about her stomach.

And made ridding herself of this exasperating man all that much more imperative.

Was it too much to hope that Dr. Bracken would take it upon himself to investigate the possibilities recorded inside the thousands of books that lined the walls? Apparently so. Throughout the vast space of the main floor and the balcony above, shelving formed semi-private nooks. Furnished with desks and chairs and bioluminescent reading lamps, students and scientists dove into the knowledge contained within the pages of books, alone or in collaboration. Five feet away stood a card catalog that would guide him. Many of the cards inside it were written and indexed by Evie herself. Not that he had ever slid a drawer open to hunt through its contents, to punch a call number into the panel of the steam attendant who would guide him on well-oiled wheels to the requested text.

Waiting for the inevitable words, she proceeded with the tedium of desk duty. Rubber stamp to ink, then to paper, making a notation of the book's return before moving on to the next. Dr. Bracken dragged in a long breath, and she braced herself. Here it came. First the flattery, then the demand for assistance.

"You're a fount of wisdom."

"I am," she agreed. No more effacing her talents, no more humbling herself so that he might preserve his own sense of self-importance. She might not be a scientist, but she *was* a trained professional and would be treated as such.

Stiffening, he rose from his casual slouch, and a faint scent reminiscent of apricots with the harsh undertones of unidentifiable laboratory chemicals wafted in her direction. Embedded in the man's very skin, the aroma followed him everywhere and was fast becoming an irritant. The deadly oleander plant he studied was in bloom yet, wisely, he'd not arrived with any of its flowers in hand.

His mustache drooped as a frown carved itself into his face. "Already students clamor to work by my side. The moment I am appointed a professor, I wish to set them to a task. Multiple projects foster a productive laboratory. I need to be ready. You *have* to help."

And so she did. Her job was to assist the scientists of Lister Laboratories in their academic endeavors. Turning Dr. Bracken away from her desk was not a possibility and, now that he'd attached himself to her, no other librarian could take her place. His devotion to her was distressingly constant.

This past fall, she'd stolen precious hours from her days to collaborate with Dr. Wilson, a chemist, laboring over the particulars of their all-but-finished joint monograph—*A Survey of Metals in Medieval Remedies, Magic or Medicine?*—a re-examination of an 1865 translation of medieval medical texts. In commentary, the translator had consigned the use of gold, silver, iron, copper and brass in formulating remedies to mere superstition, but she and Dr. Wilson argued that such metals might, by means of their impact upon catalytic enzymes—or lack thereof—be key components of the prescribed cures.

Her misfortune to have exited his office at the precise moment one Dr. Bracken ambled past.

A pretty face. A swish of skirt. A mystery he was compelled to solve. Or such had been his honeyed words. Taking it upon himself to inform Evie that he was a contender for the Hatton Chair of Chemistry, he'd followed her back to the library with a confidence so bright it had radiated throughout the reading room, turning numerous heads in their direction.

Handsome, well-dressed and rising through the ranks, she'd been flattered. At first. Before long he'd placed his self-obsession on full display and become a drain on her energy with his unwelcome advances and constant requests.

She stamped the book before her "returned" and set it aside. Resigned to the inevitable, she asked, "You wish to stay in botanicals?"

"Of course." A flicker of annoyance crossed his face. In his mind, her most important task was to remember every detail of everything he'd ever uttered. "Work proceeds apace, and I have high hopes of synthesizing oleandrin, the bioactive component of the oleander shrub, in my laboratory. Imagine the impact of such an accomplishment upon cardiac complaints. No longer will digoxin be the sole option. The future lies in broadening our undertakings to study other related bioactive compounds."

So he'd explained before. Ad nauseam.

Her ears registered naught but drivel and rubbish. If only the circulation desk was equipped with a convenient lever, that she might open a trap door, dropping him down a chute and into a waste bin.

While he waxed poetic about catalytic organic synthesis pathways, Evie glanced over his shoulder at the clock hanging upon the wall. Where was Mr. Lockwood? Not only did they need to catch Mr. Davies this holiday eve, when the dour head librarian might be moved to squash his inner Scrooge and approve their project, but she wanted to tell him about a donation carted into the library just this morning.

A patron disposing of his wealthy uncle's medical manuscript collection had placed in the library's care five large crates filled with several rare and unusual manuscripts. And the accompanying paperwork indicated that a number of the books were medicinal plant references!

Though there were other tasks that must come first, her fingers itched to lift a crowbar. What novel discoveries awaited them? Her stomach quivered with excitement. Might one contain mention of *amatiflora*, a newly discovered medicinal plant growing on the banks of the Thames? The task of combing the scientific literature for any reference to its medicinal properties had landed on

Mr. Lockwood's shoulders... and brought him to her library. A most serendipitous event.

Each time they met to work, he presented her with various botanical treats plucked from the rooftop greenhouse. A bundle of lavender. A sweet lemon. A fig. When December arrived, a twist of ivy was followed by a holly branch with bright, red berries.

Alas, no mistletoe or kisses. Not yet.

It was time to take things into her own hands. Her heart gave a tiny leap and fluttered at the thought of his lips brushing across hers. With the library more than half empty, could she orchestrate such an opportunity today?

"Absolutely fascinating," she murmured, only half-listening. Little of what Dr. Bracken said made any sense, save that he considered himself a genius at designing multistep organic synthesis processes. It was a lofty and a tenuous position to believe oneself incapable of error. The moment he encountered the slightest of impediments, she predicted a swift plummet into bitterness, an event in which she wanted no part.

Dr. Bracken reached across the desk and tugged the rubber stamp from her fingers, hanging it back upon its stand, all while letting his gaze drop to her lips. He stopped short of waggling his eyebrows, but only just. "Take me in the stacks, Miss Brown."

Evie's mind cringed at the double-entendre. There was no chance of that. She'd sooner kiss a kraken. Not that he hadn't tried to force one upon her. She was tired of side-stepping his wandering hands, but any complaint to her superiors would only be dismissed as evidence of "delicate sensibilities" and lead them to question the wisdom of hiring women. Which was why she did her best to keep a desk between them. She could handle Dr. Bracken. Papa and his airship crew had seen to that.

Next time she'd bloody his nose.

For the moment, she wished only to hustle him on his way.

"How lucky you are today." Certain he'd not yet read the medieval text that had been the focus of her scholarship for the better part of a year, she lifted a finger. Perhaps a hint of preferential treatment would mollify him. If only it would also encourage him to read. Alone. "If you'll permit me a moment, there's a book that's not on the shelf I think you'd find most enlightening."

Interest brightened his countenance. "Of course."

Evie escaped to the library office, where a volume of the Lister Library's copy lay upon her desk—one she kept handy as a reference for whenever she could sneak a few moments to work upon her monograph. With no hesitation, she defaced library property, peeling away the acquisition label inside the cover and tossing it aside. She'd glue it back in place later.

Returning, she placed the leather-bound tome upon the desk.

"What is this treasure?" Dr. Bracken beamed, pleased with the special treatment.

"*Leechdoms, Wortcunning and Starcraft of Early England* by Oswald Cockayne. This volume is a modern translation of the *Lacnunga*, an eleventh century Anglo-Saxon medical text."

He frowned.

She raised a finger. "Yes, I realize it smacks of super-stition, but there are researchers who are finding nuggets of truth within its pages." A supposition that was possibly a lie, but who would know until its cures were analyzed using a modern approach? Such was her thesis. "Perhaps it will provide you with inspiration." She slid it across the wooden surface. "For example, there is a most fascinating recipe for a wen-salve, a topical cure for tumors or swellings, involving ginger and cinnamon." It hadn't worked for her father's condition, but what if its compo-nents were isolated and concentrated? It might be selfish of her, but it was not an invalid suggestion.

Hesitantly, he flipped a few pages. "Ah, but digging out those nuggets, Miss Brown."

Bells and blazes. Must she place every thought in his head? "Might I propose you investigate the different effi-cacies of fresh ginger constituents, the gingerols, as compared to the shogaols more readily found in its dried form?"

His eyebrows flew upward. "How can you know so much?"

"I read extensively." Honestly, did he know nothing about her qualifications? Well, she wouldn't be informing him of her academic pursuits. It would be a waste of breath for this was a man who struggled with the concept of an independent woman. "Would you like me to delve into the supporting literature and have all relevant materials sent to your office?"

"What an excellent plan. You're my savior." Dr. Bracken pressed a hand to his chest. "Marry me and I promise to set you up as my very own personal assistant."

CHAPTER TWO

ASH LOCKWOOD CLENCHED HIS JAW. *Over his dead body.*

His lip peeled back in a snarl, but Ash knew Lister Library was in no danger of losing the treasure that was Miss Brown.

No, *he* was in no danger of losing her.

Bracken, the bane of her existence, thought himself such the catch that he missed—or ignored—every indication that she found him repulsive. The slight wrinkle of her nose. A hastily retracted hand. The refusal to meet his gaze.

A ring burned a hole in Ash's pocket, one that he had taken great pains to hunt down, one that had cost him a good portion of his monthly salary. By virtue of his birth, the chemist possessed resources Ash could never hope to match, a fact that stuck in his craw. *Never mind.* He wanted Miss Brown for who she was, not for how she could advance his career. And, when the right moment arrived, *his* proposal would be delivered in a far less toadying manner than Bracken's public declaration.

"Impossible." Ash forced a menacing note of cheer into his voice. If the man had any sense, he'd read the challenge in Ash's eyes. "All research would grind to a halt were you to steal her away, Bracken. You couldn't possibly be so selfish."

From the dark cloud that crept across the man's face, he could indeed. Bracken smirked. "But she's so very tempting."

Miss Brown slapped a hand upon the desk. "Yet quite content in her current position with no plans, at present, to leave, should anyone care to inquire."

The faintest flicker of a shadow crossed her face, and uncertainty rippled through him. Her job here was secure, wasn't it?

Miss Brown forever worried that someone would hold her origins against her. Though most aviator's daughters were perfectly respectable, a select few had openly consorted with disreputable airship bandits in the past, flaunting society's rules aboard dirigibles and about the airship docks. Brazen. Immoral. Shameless. Such were the words that inflamed and colored public opinion.

Only recently, with the rise of luxury airships and the elegant uniforms forced upon their public-facing employees, had opinions begun to shift. Miss Brown counted herself lucky upon that last front. She might be an aviator's daughter, but her father had risen in the ranks to captain a grand airship for Captain Oglethorpe's Luxury Airways. Instead, her greatest concern was that someone would delve yet further into the past, that they might discover her father had spent his misbegotten youth as an airship pirate, raiding East India Company airships laden with luxuries.

The revelation of such a secret *would* soil her reputation.

"My apologies." Chastened, Ash bowed, then produced a sprig of Norway fir tied with a red velvet ribbon from behind his back. "Happy Christmas."

Gratifying, the sullen look Bracken shot this gift.

As was the way Miss Brown's eyes danced. His gaze slipped ever so slightly, for it was impossible not to notice —or so he told himself—the festive nature of her close-fitting jacket, embroidered as it was with twists of ivy.

She accepted his peace offering and tucked the branch into a mercury glass vase among the ivy and holly. "Thank you. The three together make a delightful holiday arrangement." She stroked a fingertip over the soft needles of the pine branch, then met his gaze with such heat that his trousers grew tight.

Ash fought an urge to tug at his collar.

"Very professional of you, Lockwood," Bracken grouched, "to leave behind the mistletoe."

Were they that obvious? It was all he'd thought about for weeks. Yes, he'd purchased a sprig of mistletoe. Almost tied it with the velvet bow. Holding such an item aloft to kiss Miss Brown in the reading room of the

Lister Institute was untenable, but he had plans for tomorrow.

"Mistletoe isn't well-suited to a vase." He fought back a smirk.

Reading intent in Ash's eyes, Bracken's fingers curled into fists. Was he planning to present her with an overpriced trinket tomorrow in an attempt to upstage his rival? The man's glare drilled into Ash's forehead. "Good. Be certain it stays in the greenhouse."

Confirmation that the man *did* intend to pursue Miss Brown's hand.

"Have you observed any mistletoe growing while attending to your oleander bushes?" It was impossible to keep the disdain from his voice. The chemist had visited the rooftop greenhouse but once. Believing himself above the other employees in his laboratory, he'd sent a technician to collect branches, leaves and flowers. "No. For mistletoe requires a tree with substantial roots. It's *parasitic* in nature." *Not unlike yourself.* "And our container-grown trees would suffer were we to attempt to cultivate *Viscum album* indoors."

"Gentlemen," she hissed. "This is not the place. You grow loud and are attracting attention. If we might attend to library business." Turning her back on Ash, she addressed Bracken. "Ginger spice?"

"And all that's nice?" The odious man had the gall to wink. "Indeed. I look forward to reading your recommended text and greatly anticipate all associated materials."

"Excellent." She lowered her voice. "Now keep in mind, this particular book has yet to be accessioned. Most patrons are not afforded such privileges." Bracken lapped up the indulgence, and Ash frowned. "Take great care of it. I'm sure we'll have much to discuss once you've read the passage and—"

BOOM!

The floor beneath their feet heaved, then settled with a shudder.

Miss Brown's hands flew outward, bracing her arms atop the desk, eyes wide. "Crack a teacup!" Shock drove the decorum from her voice and turned it salty. "What was that?"

Ash choked back a snort as Bracken's mouth dropped in horror. Not in response to the blast—for an odd light had sparked in his eyes at the sound—but to the proper librarian's reaction. Curious, to see a man so disturbed by a woman's choice of words in the wake of *an explosion.* Still, this was not the time for comment. "Come!" He held out a hand to Miss Brown. "Aether forbid the building has caught fire."

Already other library patrons abandoned books to rush from the reading room. Fire and smoke *and* toxic fumes were significant and real dangers in a research facility.

Snatching up a familiar dog-eared brown paper notebook and clutching it to her chest like the treasure it was, Miss Brown allowed him to steady her as, amidst others, they raced down a wide staircase. A pungent chemical smell met their noses, hurrying them ever faster.

The stairs took a bend, dumping them into the building's foyer and a nightmare. Beside him, Miss Brown jerked to a stop. His own stomach churned, but it was impossible to look away. Scorched pits marred the walls, the ceiling and the floor. The large Lucifer lamp that graced the entryway had shattered, its luminous contents dripping onto the black-and-white checkered tiles of the floor to mix with blood and shattered glass. Ash counted three victims. First aid was already being given to two men who were dazed and wheezing yet largely unscathed. A third victim—missing a leg—lay motionless and beyond help in a pool of his own blood.

"Enemy attack!"

"Breach of the facility!"

"Attempted sabotage!"

His eyebrows furrowed. Whatever it was, it wasn't a laboratory accident.

Behind them, Bracken let out a strangled cry. He elbowed his way through the crowd gathered upon the stairs, surged across the floor, and dropped onto his knees beside the dead man. "No!"

Ash wouldn't have thought the chemist capable of such strong feelings. Well, not ones that would move him to disregard the damage to his trousers.

"Aether, that's Dr. Wilson!" Miss Brown gasped. "Only yesterday we met to discuss revisions to our paper." Her hand flew to her mouth, and wide eyes met his gaze. Her next words emerged as a whisper. "He never so much as hinted at his involvement, but I've heard rumors that he's a Queen's agent."

Information that cast this disaster in an entirely new light. He wrapped an arm about her shoulders and pulled her shaking form tight against his side. Was it awful of him to enjoy the soft press of her body in the wake of such a disaster, when there might well be intentional malice afoot? Guilt threatened to raise its head.

"Excuse me. Pardon." Two men pushed through the crowds. "Step aside."

One was a uniformed Lister guard. The other a man of average height and build, one averse to drawing attention. His very presence escalated suspicion of the disaster spread before them.

"Isn't that Mr. Black?" Miss Brown breathed. "He's the—"

"Queen's agent who brought the *amatiflora* to the greenhouse." Such was the name given to the new medicinal plant recently discovered growing upon the banks of the Thames. The mystery of its bloom had brought him into the library to comb the scientific literature for prior references. Within its walls he'd also found a woman who would captivate his mind and steal his heart.

A hushed murmur arose as the two men examined the scene.

The guard conferred with Mr. Black, then turned to wave his arms. "Please, if everyone will turn back, clear the premises, and go about your business. We have a fatality and must focus upon a thorough investigation as to the cause of the explosion."

The crowd heaved. Shuffled. Churned. Some began to exit, no doubt to carry away news of the disaster as far and as fast as they could possibly manage. Many continued to stare with blatant disregard for orders.

"Miss Brown," Mr. Davies snapped.

Ash dropped his arm from her shoulders, irritated that the man made him feel guilty for offering a simple comfort. "Sir." He inclined his head in greeting.

Mr. Davies ignored him.

"The feminine inclination to gossip, or so you assured me when hired, was not something to which you would succumb." The head librarian's expression was pinched, as if his shoes were too tight. "Was such a statement fiction? If not, cease your whispers and return to duty as instructed. The library doors have been left wide open. There is no lingering or immediate threat, save to the books that have been placed under our protection."

"Yes, sir." She straightened. Only the slightest quiver of her chin hinted at the effort it took to set aside her distress at the sudden and horrible death of a colleague.

Ash climbed the stairs beside her, hoping his presence offered her at least a little comfort.

Miss Brown swallowed and glanced at him. "Did Dr. Bracken's behavior strike you as odd?" Her eyebrows drew together. "Such melodrama. Certainly, they're colleagues, but I always had the impression that they didn't much care for each other. Perhaps that was only because they are—were—both candidates for the Hatton Chair of Chemistry."

"It does." For a tendril of suspicion wound its way through his gut, though there was no identifying the seed from which it sprouted. A colleague dead upon the floor and still the chemist needed the limelight to shine upon him. "I have every confidence Mr. Black's investigations will unearth whatever is amiss, be it foul play or otherwise. The Queen's agents won't be distracted by any histrionics."

They reached the library, and Miss Brown slid back behind her desk. Only a handful of patrons had returned. "Nonetheless," she pinched the bridge of her nose between her fingers, "it is an event that Dr. Bracken will exploit. Soon, he'll once again lean upon my desk, seeking sympathy for the death of a colleague."

A low growl slipped unchecked from his throat. "I'll not have it."

"And what claim have you?" A teasing light ignited in her eyes. An invitation to lighten the grim atmosphere that threatened the few remaining hours until the holiday officially began.

"None." Her words illuminated the inadequacy of his slow-paced courtship. "Yet. But my feelings for a certain librarian have become rather deep-rooted of late." He let the corner of his mouth kick up. "Unless you feel it crosses professional lines, might I offer you a private tour of a certain rooftop garden?"

Her green eyes softened. Would that he could sweep

her off her feet and carry her to the greenhouse this very minute.

A moment later starch snapped into her spine and her voice sobered. "I'm afraid it does, Mr. Lockwood."

His heart began to sink—but was tossed a life jacket by the arrival of her superior.

"Mr. Lockwood." Mr. Davies pressed his palms flat against the desk's surface and slid his gaze down his long nose to fix upon the evergreen arrangement in the vase. "While we are on the topic of gardens, I must ask that you refrain from bringing further vegetation into the reading room." His lips twisted. "Water poses a hazard to our collection."

"Apologies, sir." Miss Brown's ears burned red. "I didn't think a little decor—"

"Clearly." Mr. Davies scowled. "See it removed at closing, Miss Brown." He glanced at the stack of books awaiting her attention, then turned to peer at Ash over the top of his spectacles. "Have you everything you require, sir?"

"No, actually."

Miss Brown slid the brown notebook across the desk to him. Though a joint project, they'd agreed he would frame it as his own.

Ash kept the request formal. "I've a promising project that might be something of an imposition and wished to direct my request to you."

The older librarian nodded. "Go on."

"With the new Lister building at Kew Gardens

complete and ready to house the larger specimen plants, the original greenhouse above the east wing is now empty. As it is a relatively small enclosure, the committee has decided it will house a specialized collection of plants. I have been asked to submit a proposal." If chosen, he would also receive a promotion and a raise. But he was not the only botanist vying for the honor.

"And this involves the library how?" Doubt drew Mr. Davies's eyebrows together.

Ash leaned closer and lowered his voice. "This must remain confidential."

Mr. Davies sniffed. "We who serve Lister scientists are not in the habit of chattering about our clients' work."

So much for the enticement of secrecy. Lifting the notebook, he tried a new tactic. "With Miss Brown's assistance, I've begun studying the library's collection of pharmacopeia—from the Roman through the medieval period—cross-referencing the patterns of ingredients and associated conditions between books—mining the data, so to speak, that we might determine which plants are most likely to contain bioactive substances. Those plants deemed of the most medicinal, chemical or industrial value would then be cultivated, permitting them to easily embark upon new scientific inquiries."

"An ambitious project, Mr. Lockwood. Though interesting, our staff already has significant duties. I'm not certain I wish to impose upon them further."

Miss Brown cleared her throat. "If I may, Mr. Davies."

The head librarian sighed. "Yes?"

"Though an extensive proposition, to my knowledge such a compilation has never been undertaken. Given our substantial collection of such texts, we are uniquely positioned to assist. Not only might such a project prove invaluable, if chosen the library's status would rise in the eyes of the Lister Institute. No longer would we merely be a resource, we would be a research partner. With such a designation, you, Mr. Davies, would be appointed a position upon the Oversight Committee."

The head librarian's eyes flew open. "Well. That would be... most impressive." As a hunger for status tightened its grip, Ash could almost hear the librarian's brittle bones crackle and snap as his scrawny frame straightened. "When is this proposal due?"

"The review committee convenes in mid-January to evaluate all plans," Ash replied. "I intend to present a cross section of the data we have compiled and detail its potential use."

"For example," Miss Brown said, "a list of plants with known or suspected antibacterial properties correlated to the ingredients of specific infections to which they have been traditionally applied. Easily tested against microbes grown in a Petri dish."

"Or," Ash held her gaze a moment, "given the limited success our surgeons have treating various cancers, a list of plants which have been used to formulate wen-salves, topical treatments for tumors. A more complicated project, but one our scientists are more than capable of addressing."

Tears welled in Miss Brown's eyes, and sympathy tightened his throat. Aiding her search was the least he could do.

She had a vested interest in this project, for her father was afflicted with a skin carcinoma, one—the physicians believed—precipitated by his many years upon an airship's deck beneath the intense rays of the sun. Together they'd teased out a number of odd cures, none of which had yet proven successful. Granted more time, he hoped to delve into more obscure references, scouring ancient texts for any long-forgotten treatments.

"I suppose you wish to continue working with Miss Brown?" Mr. Davies' words betrayed a certain reluctance.

Did he suspect a budding romance? Wish to squash such an undignified emotion within the library's hallowed walls?

Ash refused to give him the chance. He kept his words carefully formal. "Two months of Miss Brown's assistance has revealed her to have an exceptional knowledge base from her time at Girton College. Going forward, particularly as we examine original texts, her knowledge of Old English will provide us with a distinct advantage."

Case presented, Ash held his breath while Mr. Davies weighed the costs and benefits of such a project. Would the lure of greater glory win over his concerns?

Miss Brown's hands shook as she stamped a book returned and set it aside.

"Mmm." The head librarian tapped his lips. "I suppose I can spare Miss Brown for an hour in the evenings. Two, if she's willing to forgo her lunch hour."

"Thank you, Mr. Davies," she said.

Ash let out an exhale.

The head librarian pinned them both with a cautionary stare. "This is a *professional* arrangement. Do not make me regret my decision." Mr. Davies scanned the reading room before him, noted the paucity of patrons due to the impending holiday and gave a great sigh. Little more than an hour remained until closing. "You might as well start now."

CHAPTER THREE

A SANCTIONED EXCUSE TO SPEND more time with Mr. Lockwood. A declaration of his interest after two months of flirting. *Two!* With the near-empty library, Evie intended to make the most of this rare opportunity. Pages flipped inside her stomach. A private tour of the greenhouse? She wouldn't turn down that offer. Not that she was willing to wait for him to lead her down a garden path. Winning permission to work upon their project during work hours required a celebration. And while the leafy concealment of arbors held their appeal, libraries too had their own semi-private passageways lined with the tall magnificence of books.

As they passed their usual study nook, Evie glanced over her shoulder and threw Ash a cheeky smile, pleased to find a sparkle of appreciation in his eyes as his gaze followed the sway of her hips. Her new green walking dress, though a serviceable wool—as befitted a librarian—

was carefully tailored to set off her figure and entice the eyes of a certain botanist, *not* a chemist. It was no accident that the collar and lapels of the jacket were embroidered with a trailing vine, that they parted beneath her chin to expose a white blouse with tiny, pearl buttons, a blouse nipped in at the waist by a darker green cincher, before the pleats and folds of her bustled skirts flared, falling gently to ankle length.

A sharp turn between a long run of bookshelves drew them into shadows, away from the eyes of any lingering patrons. She stopped and hooked a finger atop the spine of a book. "Ought we include Culpeper's unauthorized work, the *Complete Herbal and English Physician?* Completed in 1653, it would take us beyond the medieval period, but I admire how he was a radical thinker for his time, unafraid of a hint of scandal." A long, bold glance from beneath her eyelashes encouraged Mr. Lockwood to take advantage of their momentary seclusion.

As he reached for the book, she didn't move—a bold act that brought him so close that she was certain he could hear her heart pounding. Excitement and desire heightened by the possibility of discovery left her breathless.

He dropped a warm hand atop hers. "Is this an invitation, Miss Brown?" The rough pad of his thumb stroked over her skin. Ripples of heat spread outward.

"It's an opportunity," her voice was a hushed whisper, "to uncover any chemistry between us." Would he kiss her? Ought she tug on his cravat? It always hung loose about his throat in defense against the heat and humidity of the greenhouse, a welcome habit that provided her with a tantalizing glimpse of the hollow of his throat. She settled for dropping the flat of her palm upon his chest, gratified to feel his own heart hammering against his rib cage. "One you seem determined to waste."

With a huff of soft laughter, he tipped her chin up with his fingers and closed the distance between them.

Evie rocked forward onto her toes, inhaling his woodsy scent, one that had driven her to distraction these long few weeks. She was more than halfway in love with the man.

His mouth caught hers, soft at first, as his lips explored the shape of hers, then grew bolder, inching toward a demand. *More*, her body begged. Fire raced across her skin, stealing her breath. But she felt him hesitate, begin to retreat. *Too soon!* She wanted more. Darting her tongue against his lips, Evie reminded him she was no shy, delicate hothouse flower. No, she was an aviator's daughter, a hearty bloom with no reputation to protect.

A stifled groan escaped his throat a moment before he sealed his lips to hers, delving his tongue inside her mouth with bold strokes. He tasted of rainwater and peppermint, an intoxicating combination that failed to quench a burning need inside her. Pure oxygen fed a bed of coals. Feverish and weak-kneed, her hand fisted upon his waistcoat.

Reason insisted that they stop.

But this kiss exceeded her every hope, and so she shoved the sensible admonishment aside and kissed him back, pouring passion onto the fire.

His hands caught at the embroidered lapels of her jacket. Fingers slid behind their folds while thumbs traced the winding path of the vines downward, twisting and writhing across her chest, over the slope of her breasts. He tugged her closer, swallowing the gasp that escaped her throat when his teasing fingers brushed over the peaked tips of her nipples, when the delightful friction stoked the flames yet higher.

Dangerous, this heat between the shelves, with so much dry paper available as kindling.

And yet she uncurled her fingers and reached for his cravat—

Without warning, his hands gripped her waist, pushed her down onto her heels and away from his warmth. Her eyes flew open. "Why—"

Nearby, footsteps echoed in the stacks. A patron wandering about, searching for a book. Alarm raced down her spine.

He held out a hand. "Pass me a book," he demanded, breathless. A lock of hair had tumbled over his forehead and color darkened his cheeks. "Books. Stack them upon my arms and quickly. We've been out of sight for far too long."

Her hand still gripped the spine of *The London*

Dispensatory. She pulled the text free and dropped it into his hands.

"More, Miss Brown. Anything remotely relevant."

Focused now, she yanked a number of books from the shelf and stacked them upon his outstretched arms. He turned and strode away, leaving her amidst the books, heart pounding. She pressed hands against her overheated cheeks and dragged in a deep breath. Then smiled. Such wanton behavior.

And she regretted none of it.

SEATED at their usual reading table, Ash forced himself to convey every impression of serious scholarship. He cracked open the brown notebook, flipped to a fresh page and snatched up a pen. By rote, he scratched out the names of all plants known for their use as eye salves, willing away the ache of denied pleasure that still flooded his body. But the list was barely legible. His grip on the blameless fountain pen was too tight, and his mind refused to concentrate on anything save the memory of Evie's curves, the faint taste of spun sugar upon her lips, the soft whimper of protest as he broke their kiss.

With her invitation, Miss Brown had turned all his plans upside down. He tugged the ring he'd purchased from his pocket. Between his fingers, the dull gold band glowed in the bioluminescent lamplight. Impatience urged him to drop onto one knee, to propose this very minute so that they might spend the entirety of the holiday celebrating. Prudence advocated for a private moment, one more favorable to romance.

He shoved the ring back in his pocket.

Where was she? He struggled not to glance over his shoulder. He'd left her standing in the stacks. Abruptly. Callously. But, by aether, the urge to ravish her among her beloved books had been overwhelming. They weren't alone, not even remotely, and he had no business letting his hands wander over her sweet form. Not here.

Before him, the balcony provided a grand view of the vaulted reading room below. Only a few dedicated souls remained. Many had closed their texts and slipped from the library, heading home on a cold, December evening to settle into a cozy holiday with family. Tomorrow the library was closed, as were the other offices and facilities of the Lister Institute. A rare day when all activities on the campus ground to a complete halt. Almost. For it was impossible to keep all scientists from their laboratories.

Or him from his greenhouse. His own parents were miles upon miles north in Boroughbridge, celebrating with his sisters and brothers and nieces and nephews. Proud of his work, they nonetheless struggled to comprehend how he could find happiness in such a crowded, hazy city. But they'd not yet laid eyes upon the amazing glass and iron houses that arched above the roofs of the Lister Institute, where plants from around the globe flourished, where scientists strove to unlock various botanical mysteries. True, some ten miles removed from the institute, a larger facility had been built upon the grounds of Kew Gardens and many from his department now vied for the honor of moving to a more rural setting. But London—and one particular librarian—had captured his heart.

The air shifted—carrying a hint of honeysuckle soap —a moment before Miss Brown deposited a new stack of books upon their table and slid into the chair beside him.

"Thank you," she breathed. "For emphasizing the potential for wen-salves. I'd tell you Papa would be thrilled to learn of our minor victory on his behalf, but when you meet him tomorrow, you'll find that he defines grumpy, old patriarch."

"Still resistant to your ministrations?"

"Always." She huffed. "The skin lesion has continued to spread. He's taken to wearing a mask and is refusing all further surgeries. Under protest and only because I'm his daughter does he submit to my herbal concoctions."

"We'll keep looking," he reassured her. Her father's condition was, after all, the inspiration for their project.

When Ash arrived at the library under Mr. Thistleton's orders to comb the texts for any reference to *amatiflora*, a medicinal plant known only to gypsies, he'd discovered most of the old herbals stacked upon Miss Brown's desk. During stolen moments and after hours, she was hunting for a remedy that might treat her father's malignant skin lesion. They'd soon struck up a working relationship and, though she'd been handing various formulas to a local chemist, he'd taken over the task of compounding the various botanical ointments and creams in the stillroom adjacent to the greenhouse.

A few remedies had shown initial promise, then gradually lost their efficacy. Most did nothing. Possibly because the reference assumed a trained, experienced practitioner and offered no measurements, leaving them guessing at the various quantities and ratios of ingredients to incorporate. But neither of them voiced aloud the possibility that no such cure existed, within the ancient manuscripts or without. Miss Brown refused to give up.

She was a woman that any man would be lucky to have at his side.

Would that he, a gardener's son, be able to win her.

The dalliance of the lord's youngest son with Mary, the vicar's daughter Ash had been courting, had resulted in a fraught situation—one resolved by a hasty marriage and a distant military posting—and the lord's offer to smooth the path of Ash's future by offering him an advanced education. Reeling from the revelation that Mary had been accepting his attentions only to cover her dalliance with another, Ash—bitter and disappointed—had snatched at the chance to expand his world.

It had been exactly the push he'd needed.

Though he had graduated from Victoria University of Manchester, he'd disappointed everyone by earning a degree in botany, rather than engineering, and by heading to London, rather than by returning to apply his knowledge in the lord's service.

Hard work and not a small amount of luck had

earned him the title Research Assistant at the Lister Institute. Without this project, without earning a more advanced degree, there he would stay.

But he had plans. Ones in which Miss Brown featured prominently.

From the passion she'd poured into their kiss, he hoped she might have similar designs. Yet, beside him, she'd fallen silent, her eyes fixed upon a single page as if the words upon them blurred and ran together.

Ash slid his left hand beneath the table to catch at her fingers, careful to keep his gaze directed at the notebook before him. "Have I shocked you?"

"Not at all." Her lips twitched as she threaded her fingers through his. "You know of my past, that I'm no innocent."

He did. Once she'd been engaged and, by society's standards, her conduct ought to have seen her married. She'd shared that particular secret from her past when his courtship became clear. "I see no reason for that to mean I should treat you with less respect."

"Ah." Evie hummed. "I'm glad to hear it. Though I must admit to a certain frustration requiring a drastic step to entice you to act."

He huffed a soft laugh, gratified that he didn't suffer alone. "It's true, I'd planned to be more circumspect." Sliding a finger beneath the cuff of her sleeve, he traced a path across the delicate interior of her wrist.

Her breath caught.

A risky glance revealed heat creeping into her cheeks,

and his mind began entertaining a number of fantasies about how else his touch might inflame her desire.

"About your botanical family," she ventured, sliding him a coy glance. "Am I to be introduced tomorrow?"

The only day they could hope to be entirely alone. He quirked an eyebrow. "So you *do* wish to cross that line?"

"Did I not make that clear a few minutes past? Weeks of botanical gifts have whet my appetite for an invitation to enter your greenhouse. Where," her hand crept onto his thigh, "one might, presumably, find a vine-covered arbor in the dead of winter." A bold and forward statement to match her touch.

The sensation of her palm skimming over the wool of his trousers sent blood rushing back into his groin. Was she determined to drive him mad? "A grave oversight that I intend to rectify immediately. Tomorrow, then, after Christmas dinner?" Risking censure, he leaned closer and whispered, his voice rough and raw. "I have every interest in peeling those vines of yours away to explore what lies beneath."

Gratifying, the way his words made her hand tighten upon his thigh and her next words emerge as a breathy whisper. "I look forward to entertaining your rising expectations. I do hope they are... substantial."

Ash choked and nearly swallowed his tongue. He caught at her hand before she attempted an investigation. Aether, he was about to spontaneously combust.

"Will you let me escort you home this evening?"

Perhaps there might be mistletoe hanging in her home. Not that a few chaste kisses in her family's home would do anything to cool his ardor. The sooner Ash spoke with her father, the better.

"My sister isn't expecting you until tomorrow," she demurred. The light of her features dimmed. "With the exuberance of six nephews whirling about tonight, there'll be nothing but chaos and confusion. And the evening will be bittersweet. Mum and her Christmas expectations were always... weighty. Papa will be lowering the level of household rum, and my sister won't yet have run through her baking stores. She'll likely carry on past midnight. It's best we don't add to the chaos."

Disappointment dragged his stomach to his knees. A cold grate and an empty room waited for him at his boarding house. But he understood why she would not force her sister to play hostess, to feign a false joy for unexpected company.

Enlightenment broke. All those long hours spent bent over her many books of late? A way to hide from the pain of losing her mother during the holiday season. Five years past. And so soon after the death of her fiancé.

Hard to regret Miss Brown's subsequent availability, but he *was* sorry that she'd endured such pain. An airship engineer, he recalled. For a vast sum, the boy—for he'd been all of nineteen—had signed aboard a ship known to travel dangerous routes. Presumed lost to the Carpathian air bandits, none of the crew had ever been heard from again.

In the adjacent alcove, pages rustled. A reminder that they were not at all alone. He gave her hand a squeeze, then released it. As her warm touch slid away, he found himself bereft.

Evie cleared her throat and nudged her leg against his. "Now, about this project of ours. It's pure brilliance, and it's time the committee learned about it." Her voice held a note of false cheer. "Remember, despite our presentation to Mr. Davies, I want equal credit for all the work. We'll either rocket to fame together, or we'll both sink back into academic obscurity."

"Never fear, you'll make your mark in the field of medieval herbals." Time to focus. There was much to accomplish before they would be ready to present to the review committee. "Prestige will be ours."

KISSING IN THE LIBRARY.

He'd caught the faintest glimpse of them through the screen of books. A disgusting display of lust, and it burned low in his gut that Miss Brown had succumbed to the gardener's charms. What was Lockwood but some peasant's son who'd grown up in a cottage with dirt floors?

He was of the aristocracy. Wealthy and well-bred. But for the unfortunate gender of his mother, the title viscount would have passed to him. Though the family estate now descended through his cousin, as was lawful, he was not without resources. Mother had a generous annuity and was in good health. His own investments in Captain Oglethorpe's Luxury Airways kept the coffers brimming. And eventually, the London townhome would pass to him.

As a spouse, he was by far the better choice.

Alas, it appeared he must educate Miss Brown as to the error of her ways. All he needed were a few private minutes of her time.

Impatient, he'd waited for the library to empty of its patrons, its librarians.

True to form, Miss Brown was among the last to leave. He started forward, then stopped and frowned. Lockwood was among the knot of stragglers.

Perhaps it was for the best, what with the blood and grime that marred the knees of his trousers. He'd change first. Approach her later. Then rip out the roots of this budding romance.

Bracken hung back in a shadowed alcove of the hall-way, watching as Miss Brown pulled a great iron key— such poor security—from her pocket to lock the library's carved, wooden door. Too many were careless, even those who worked in secured laboratories.

Lockwood walked at her side as they exited the build-ing. Together. Careful to retain an appropriate space between them. Even so, he cast her lustful glances, no doubt entertaining improper thoughts about the rights that would be his once he slipped that ridiculous ring onto her finger.

Copper, if he had to guess. Likely to turn her skin green. Such a band was far too simple, too common. Faceted gemstones ought to grace his fiancée's hand. A cut-glass bottle with a gold atomizer ought to perfume the air that surrounded her, not a simple cluster of holiday greenery that could be purchased on any street corner.

He could do better.

He *would* do better. He would secure her as his muse. A holiday present to himself, along with a clear path to the Hatton Chair. With her at his side, bound to him, her access to knowledge at his disposal, academic honors and recognition would be his. Smiling, he stroked his mustache, twisting its end about his finger.

He watched from the doorway of the Lister Institute as Miss Brown's better sense returned. She waved off Lockwood's attentions, choosing to board an omnibus that would carry her home.

Good. With the gardener out of the way, it was time. He'd stop by his townhome, change, and collect an appropriate engagement ring before paying Miss Brown a formal call. Imagine her joy when he graced her parlor with his company on Christmas Eve, then bent upon one knee to declare his undying affection.

CHAPTER FOUR

"Hurry, Aunt Evie!" Four small boys cried, immediately countermanding their order by throwing their arms about her knees and ankles.

Delightful smells wafted from the warm kitchen. Flour and yeast. Cinnamon and sugar. Nutmeg and cloves. All recalling many happy memories of holidays past, if tinged with a touch of sadness. Evie smiled. Feeding *six* grandsons would have filled Mum's heart to overflowing. Though they wouldn't remember, each of the eldest three had made quite the mess gumming Grandma's iced biscuits on past Christmas Eves. A tradition their mother clung to, never deviating from the recipe.

A prick of sadness threatened to bring tears to her eyes.

"Why the hurry?" She pretended ignorance as she

tugged off her gloves, unable to so much as unbutton her coat amidst the swirl of nephews that engulfed her in the foyer.

Timmy, at the advanced age of nine, hung back. He feigned a quiet dignity, but strategy danced in his eyes. He'd already shifted in the direction of the kitchens, ready to race his siblings in a mad dash to reach the treats first, certain of his victory. "Mum said we can't touch the gingerbread—"

"Or pies! Or tarts!"

Timmy sighed. "Or the pies and tarts, until you've taken the first bite."

The holiday baking was extensive. A time when her sister, Beatrix, would tie on an apron and disappear into the kitchens for a full week. The steam cook and various implements that kept a family of ten fed, would be pushed beyond their design specifications, baking around the clock to churn out a feast fit for kings. Though most treats were off limits until Christmas Day.

"Well then." She ruffled silky curls. "You know how this works. Who has it?" A grubby hand waved in the air. "A crust? Without even a hint of filling?" She feigned exasperation as she plucked the pastry fragment from Joey's fingers and sniffed. Currents. Candied orange peel. Cinnamon. And hints of so many others met her nose. "It must be mincemeat!"

"You guessed!"

"Well, then. Are you ready?" Her nephews released her legs. "Set. Go!" The moment she bit down, the boys bolted. Pushing and shoving and laughing, they tumbled through the door into the kitchens.

She hung up her coat and carefully placed the vase of gifted cuttings of greenery upon the hall table. A small offering beside the swags of garlands that were tied to the railings with red, velvet ribbons. Alone for the moment, she permitted herself to indulge in the memory of Mr. Lockwood's delicious kiss, of his hands brushing over her. A feverish flutter stirred deep inside her. Tomorrow, during her private tour of his leafy domain, she intended to encourage those strong, wandering hands of his to pick up where they'd left off.

Bang! With a thump and a crash, the kitchen door swung open. Laden with tea and stacked with individual mincemeat pies, the roving tea table wheeled past, clattering and clanking as it made its way to Papa's study.

Beatrix poked her head out. Flour dusted her cheeks and hands. "Have tea with Papa while I settle the howling pack. There's a letter for you on the tray. Rob will be back soon with the Yule log, and we'll drag everyone upstairs to the drawing room."

A letter. From Oxford? Could it be? An entirely different kind of agitation churned in her stomach. Odds were it was a rejection. The one-year visiting medieval scholarship she'd applied for, one with unfettered access to the Bodleian Library, had yet to be awarded to a woman.

Evie opened her mouth to reply but found herself facing a swinging door. Chaos would reign from here until tomorrow afternoon, when the household would fall into a postprandial stupor. But only a brief one. A household filled with so many rambunctious boys was rarely quiet.

Best to rip open the missive, swallow the contents in one gulp, then let go of the fantasy. Easy enough to lose herself in the distractions of home, work... and Mr. Lockwood.

Why, then, did her heart hammer so loudly?

Nothing to do but have done with it. Avoiding the words inked within the missive would only give her indigestion. She hung up her coat and, hand pressed to her stomach, entered Papa's study.

Here one always expected Lucifer lamps to swing as the floor bobbed and weaved beneath one's feet, all while balloon and mooring tethers twisted and snapped in unexpected gusts of wind. In front of the window, a helm salvaged from a confiscated pirate's airship was affixed to the floor, a quiet nod to Papa's early days as a sky bandit. From hooks nailed to the wall hung several stratospheric oxygen masks and wing packs, near at hand for any crisis requiring a swift evacuation.

Every so often, his grandsons would invade. Timmy would lift the tarnished spyglass to his eye, ordering his brothers to steer the house toward the distant sliver of sky visible above the townhomes across the street. All would be smooth sailing at first, but, invariably, the airship would come under attack and evasive maneuvers would be required. A blunderbuss dragged from a brass-bound trunk and a pair of dull cutlasses liberated from the wall would hold back air pirates while futile attempts would be made to lift an old cannon ball that sat in the corner.

In the center of the room squatted two old and battered armchairs, one of which was occupied by the windblown airship captain himself. Papa held a cup of rum in his hand. Beside him upon a scarred wooden cask rested an empty tin cup, and the scent of tobacco hung in the air. Weathered airmen were forever dropping by for a chat. For advice. Papa had done well for himself and invested wisely.

"Ah, my scholar returns." Papa smiled, half of his mouth hidden by the thin cotton mask he'd taken to wearing to hide the ulcerated and spreading cancerous skin lesion. His eyes searched her hands for a bottle or a jar. "No new herbal concoction?"

"Not yet." Hands unsteady, she snatched up the letter from the roving tea table. Sinking into a still-warm chair, she injected her voice with an optimism she no longer felt. "But soon." Though he rolled his eyes, she poured him a cup of tea and set it beside him along with a mincemeat pie. "You need to eat. And to drink something that won't pickle your liver."

"And you need to open that letter before your face permanently wears that expression. I can almost hear the alarm bells. From Oxford is it? Took them long enough."

She tore into the envelope, unfolded the paper and froze at the words upon the page.

"Well?"

"Accepted," she whispered. Internally, several organs came unmoored. "For Hilary term."

A rejection would have made life choices easy, but this... The luxury of developing her very own research project under the guidance of a mentor? An entire year with nothing to focus upon save her own research?

Her heart leapt into her throat, even as her stomach flipped and dropped to her knees. The entirety of her internal organs were on the verge of rebellion.

Beatrix already managed the household circus unaided, but Evie couldn't leave Papa. He needed her, needed her working on a cure. And what of her project with Mr. Lockwood? It was a rare thing for a librarian to be granted permission to work upon a research project during business hours. And what of the man himself who kissed her as if she alone could quench the fire that burned within his chest? How could she toss such passion aside when she'd already fallen halfway in love with him?

But the Bodleian Library! If she turned Oxford down, there would never be another offer. Her heart gave a twist and slipped, falling to land beside her stomach. Perhaps its queasiness could be quelled with a bite of mincemeat pie. She snagged a pastry for herself and bit into it, but the flaky crust and rich spices on her tongue failed to work their usual magic.

"Well, then, about that gentleman caller you're expecting for Christmas dinner tomorrow. When he speaks to me, do I welcome him into the family or break the news gently?"

"You do neither." She couldn't tear her eyes from the letter. Would the correct path forward ever be clearly marked? "I'm three and twenty, Papa. Quite capable of handling this situation myself."

"Five years since Samuel was lost. Four since your mother slipped away." Papa tossed back his rum. "I've no regrets about sending you to Girton College, but it's time to move on with your life. What'll it be, Evie? Your books or a family? Either way you shouldn't be fussing over an old, dying man while your sister raises half a cricket team."

She glared at him, irritated that he continued to address his own mortality with such little care, but refused to argue with him. Not tonight.

Most thought Papa had wasted hard-earned money sending a female to college. She disagreed. But her critics were right about one thing, college had given her *ideas*. A certain kiss had generated yet more new ones. Why not a family *and* a career? She liked children, though six seemed excessive. One—perhaps two—might be manageable.

Best to proceed as if no letter had arrived. "Certain opportunities have arisen at the Lister Institute. I've no intention of leaving London."

"Stubborn child." Papa shook his head. "About these salves of yours. It's time to stop."

"What! I certainly will not. There's still—"

Her father raised a hand. "Davy dropped by." An old friend. He and Papa had risen in the ranks together. Though Davy stubbornly refused to retire, claiming the adventure kept him young. "Wants me on his next voyage."

"Absolutely not!" Evie dropped the pie back onto its plate and shot to her feet. She began to pace. "You're not deaf. You heard the doctor. You must stay out of the sun." Even with the enclosed helm of a luxury airship, there was no chance Papa would remain indoors. High in the sky and above the clouds, the sunlight was intense.

"Now, Evie. Shuttered in this room is not how I intend to spend the rest of my life, be it months or years. I've not been to Japan in a few years, and I've a mind to visit the geisha girls." He waggled his eyebrows.

"Papa!" Such was not a topic she wished to discuss with her father.

"Oh, don't look so horrified. Life is to be lived, not spent wrapped up in cotton wool." He tossed back the last of his rum and lifted a mincemeat pie. "I wasn't going to tell you until after Christmas, but as you've a man on a hook, you've not but a few days to drag him ashore if you want me to give you away. Might be I could pull some strings, acquire one of those fancy special licenses." Papa tipped his head. "Or will you follow that dream of yours to Oxford and become a distinguished professor of medieval studies?"

Her mind locked onto one word. "Days?"

Papa nodded. "We lift off in three days."

"Three." Her mouth dropped. "You're set on this?"

"I am." A certain stubbornness to his jaw told her there'd be no changing his mind.

She dragged in a deep breath. Forget making any decisions about her own future, she had only three short days left to find a cure for her father. Everything else must wait.

"Well, then." Shock petrified her words as she attempted to fill them with false cheer. "I'll be at work tonight, back at dawn to see what Father Christmas has tucked inside stockings."

"Evie—"

She held up a hand and let her voice grow firm. "Before you float away, I wish to speak with the airship's doctor. You'll leave with an assortment of treatments." Her mind flashed to the crates in the library's office. Odds were low they'd contain a Christmas miracle, but there was no way to know until they were unpacked. She certainly wouldn't find one wishing upon a Yule log. Instead, she'd do her best to hunt one down. Starting tonight.

"Stay, Evie. You ought to be at home tonight. Besides, it's not on your shoulders to produce a cure. Some things can't be fixed."

Papa was right, of course. The notion of missing one of his last evenings at home, especially Christmas Eve, weighed heavily upon her. But if she stayed, she would spend it pacing before the fire, her mind elsewhere. Better if she returned to work to examine the contents of the crates. If there was nothing noteworthy, at least her mind would be at ease.

"Don't argue. I inherited my stubbornness from you." She bent to kiss her father's forehead. "Festivities are about to commence in the drawing room, and the boys will want to know if they can expect snow tomorrow."

"My joints most certainly think so." Knowing he could do nothing to stop her, he sighed, caught at her hand and gave it a tight squeeze. "Take a warm coat, Evie."

Weary, she stuffed the letter from Oxford into her pocket, then climbed the stairs to her room, intending to change into a more serviceable dress, one better suited to sitting upon the floor midst packing material, dust and crumbling parchment. Fingers at the buttons of her collar, she sighed at the stacks of books and papers, at the fountain pen that lay abandoned beside them. Had its ink run dry? So much for her plans to spend a few hours working upon her monograph of medieval remedies over the holiday. At such a pace and with Dr. Wilson's tragic death, it would be months before she could submit her paper for publication.

Unless...

Were Papa's imminent departure and Oxford's acceptance letter signs that she ought to move on with her life? She shook her head. No. Such meaning could also be ascribed to Mr. Lockwood's declaration of interest and the approval of their project.

Though her mind raced, first contemplating one

perspective then the other, it was impossible to choose a path forward.

Outside, a steam wagon clattered to a halt and a shout went up. With a sad smile, she twitched aside the curtain to peer out the frost-edged window. From the back of a steam wagon, her brother-in-law wrestled a far-too-large damp log—one festooned in red ribbons and sprigs of holly—and hauled it indoors. A country tradition her mum had brought with her from the north and shoehorned into a city drawing room. A tradition Beatrix insisted upon continuing. For the next twelve days, her nephews would work hard to keep a yule log burning in a fireplace grate designed for coal.

Wait.

Was that—? No. Disbelief and denial competed to widen her eyes. But it was. The glow of a streetlamp illuminated Dr. Bracken as he broke away from foot traffic and approached her front door, a bouquet of hothouse flowers in hand. Grimacing, she dropped the curtain. Had his suggestion of marriage not been in jest? *Aether forbid.* On the heels of his colleague's death, he thought to press his suit?

Her stomach sank. It was impossible to reach the front door before Dr. Bracken did. One of her nephews could, even now, be escorting him into Papa's study. She cringed. Not ten minutes past, her father had suggested she might like to plan a swift wedding. Would he mistake Dr. Bracken for an over-eager holiday guest and welcome him with open arms?

Bells and blazes.

A lady wouldn't run, but if she made an appearance, Dr. Bracken would glue himself so tightly to her side that she'd never break free. Politeness would force her to play hostess and, by the time he left, it would be too late to return to the library.

There was no choice but to flee.

Evie stuffed her coin purse into her pocket, then dug into the back of her wardrobe to yank out a thick woolen coat that had seen better days. She shrugged it on and snatched up a pair of red, woolen mittens and a hat, then slipped down the back stairwell.

"Beatrix!" Evie hissed, edging into the warm kitchens.

Pots and pans and bowls and spoons were piled beside the sink. The counters were dusted with flour and sugar and spices too numerous to count. The oven ran full blast and something bubbled on the stovetop. The steam cook kneaded dough at the table while the automixer whirled away. Treats of all kinds—recently pillaged by her nephews—were stacked upon plates.

"Where on earth do you think you're going?" Her sister wiped her hands on her apron. "You've a finely dressed gentlemen caller who asked to speak with Papa." Beatrix's sing-song voice teased. "I'm willing to wager there's a ring in one of his pockets."

Evie grimaced. "*This* man's attentions are unwelcome. Scoot the self-important weasel out the door as soon as you can manage it."

"Oh?" Her sister's eyebrows rose. "I thought—"

"The extra plate I asked you to set for Christmas dinner is for a Mr. Lockwood. *Not* a Dr. Bracken."

"Oh, really?" A smile broke out across Beatrix's flour-streaked face. "*Two* men in pursuit of your hand? And one regarded with distaste and disdain. There's a story here, one full of drama and intrigue. Tell me more."

Rolling her eyes, Evie shook her head. "Later. I have to go. I left something important at work."

All humor fell away. "Evie, it's Christmas Eve *and* it's late. This can—"

"No, it can't wait."

"But Papa—"

"He knows." Ought she tell Beatrix? Yes. She deserved to know. "Papa intents to float away to Japan with Davy. They leave in three days."

"No!" Disbelief dropped her sister's jaw. "But the doctors said—"

"When has that ever stopped him?"

Beatrix's lips flattened. "And so you're going back to the library to continue your hunt for a cure. Evie, you've run yourself ragged—"

She held up a hand. "One last try. There are some new books..." Guilt trickled into her stomach as her eyes surveyed the disastrous state of the kitchens. "I'll be back at dawn to tie on an apron and do your every bidding. And," she stabbed a finger into her sister's shoulder, "you're not to lift a finger doing dishes. Leave them all for me."

"They'll be stacked to the ceiling." Beatrix pointed a finger at her. "And I intend to drag every detail out of you about this Dr. Bracken. I might even tidy up, take tea in the parlor and have a look for myself. *Two gentlemen!*"

"Careful, this one might bite." Evie snatched an iced biscuit off a plate and backed out of the kitchen door into the garden. Though cold nipped at fingertips, ears and noses, the streets were abuzz with people rushing to and fro on last minute errands. Many frantically searching out the perfect gift for a loved one.

Much like her.

CHAPTER FIVE

ASH CLOSED THE DOOR UPON the cold drafts swirling about his rented room. With no one to share his evenings with, he rarely spent any significant time in the boarding house. Why spend his hard-earned coin on coal when there was a cot tucked away in a back room of the greenhouse near the warmth of the dedicated furnace, a necessity for maintaining year-round growing conditions?

Here in London, the plants were his closest companions—and he'd spend Christmas Eve with them while making arrangements to tempt a bride. He missed his parents, brothers and sisters, as well as the holiday traditions of the north—wassails, a Yule log, evergreens dragged in from the countryside—and had torn into the package waiting for him, but a bright future with the Lister Institute beckoned. Trailing behind his father through the grand gardens for so many years had sparked his love for all things botanical, it just hadn't been enough.

Here lay opportunity.

Working together, he and Miss Brown could win the contest, elevating both the library and the greenhouse in the eyes of Lister's scientists and permitting them to tap into the genius of the men and women who worked within its many laboratories.

There was much to admire about Miss Brown herself. Imagine being able to hold so many languages—both living and dead—in one's mind that every book was a treasure trove of knowledge. He marveled at her determination and drive, at the cutting insight she brought to so many projects. Yet for all her hard work, she'd gained very little. Even when the committee chose their project —for he refused to consider the alternative—she stood only to win academic prestige, while he would secure a promotion and, with it, a more generous salary. The means to support a wife. A family.

He would do all he could to see her contribution was not forgotten, but he also hoped she might consider merging their two lives by taking him as her husband.

With the holiday underway, not another soul would be present in the greenhouse to mock the small romantic touches he had planned. Tomorrow evening, as the sun fell, he would lead Miss Brown down a magical garden path to the small arbor tucked in a corner where the glass roof sloped downward, revealing a sweeping view of

London. There, beneath an arch of passion flowers, he would lower himself onto one knee.

Aether, that kiss. Luring him behind a bookcase. Daring him to touch her. Melting beneath his lips. His heart pounded at the memory. Would that he'd declared himself weeks ago. He'd wasted far too much time, time they could have spent in each other's company outside the library. A mistake he'd not make again.

A feverish heat swept over him. During that private tour she so craved, he might make the most of their solitude. Learn the shape of her lips. Savor their taste. Permit his hands to wander without worry of discovery.

He closed his eyes and took a long, deep breath. Pointless to let his thoughts drift in such directions when it would be hours before would be in Miss Brown's presence again, and most of that in the company of her family. He was counting on the approval of her father, for family mattered very much.

Ash wrapped the new red muffler knitted by his mother about his neck and popped one of her special peppermint candies into his mouth, then stepped outside.

On this cold and blustery night, storefronts were ablaze with lights, their door chimes ringing as shoppers whisked in and out, many clutching brown-paper packages to their chests. A few paused on the pavement to turn an eye upward, predicting snow with excited voices. Street by street, Ash dodged crank hacks and steam carriages, smiling at those adorned with red bows and ivy wreaths.

Propelled by anticipation, he rounded a final corner and leapt up the Institute's broad, stone steps two at a time.

"Tonight?" The night guard was accustomed to Ash's odd hours, but still his eyebrows rose.

"No worries." Ash grinned as he pressed his hand to the security pad. "I've big plans to put in place for tomorrow."

Click. The guard waved him inside.

At the sight before him, the smile dropped from Ash's face, and the peppermint in his stomach congealed. How had today's disaster managed to slip his mind? The grim task of removing the remains, of scrubbing away the blood, had been attended to, but scorch marks still marred the tiles, the walls. Entire chunks of both were missing.

Awful. He couldn't begin to imagine the sorrow Dr. Wilson's family must be enduring this evening.

Not that *everyone* was genuinely distressed.

All about him, faces had registered shock and surprise. But that look in Bracken's eyes at the moment of the explosion... He knew something. Something he didn't wish to share.

Not that Ash had any evidence to offer.

Still, after the holiday, Ash would seek out the Queen's agent, let him know of his suspicions. Polished, pompous and privileged Bracken might be, but Mr. Black wouldn't leave any facet of a crime unexamined. If Bracken had something to hide, it wouldn't stay hidden for long.

Solemn, Ash climbed upward, arrived at the greenhouse door. Passing its security, he stepped inside. Welcome heat and humidity wrapped around him as he shed his coat. With deliberate effort he pushed aside grim notions and focused on happier thoughts.

Would the waves of Miss Brown's hair curl? Would she shed her jacket? Perhaps unfasten a pearly button or two of her collar?

With his spirits somewhat lighter, he rolled up his sleeves and set to work. She'd hinted that she wished to be led down a garden path and damned if he wasn't going to provide her with an experience no other could rival. He'd start by adding a touch of lighting...

An hour or so later, Ash stepped back and surveyed his work. He'd outdone himself. If only nature would cooperate. He turned. Now he was the one with dreams of snow, for a touch of frost to the glass plates overlooking the street below—

Was that—? He swiped away the condensation and squinted.

No.

It could not be Miss Brown stepping out of a crank hack. She was snug in her parlor, surrounded by family.

Except.

That determined walk, though admittedly concealed by a thick coat, was precisely the one he'd spent so many hours in the library admiring.

What could possibly bring her here at such an hour?

Nothing good.

He exited the greenhouse at a run, rushed down flights of stairs, intent on offering assistance or, at the very least, his company. He rounded the last bend and dashed into the hallway.

Tap. Tap. Tap. Her leather shoes tapped a course intent upon reaching the library door with all due speed. From the stiff set of her shoulders, something was very much amiss. "Miss Brown!" he called, forcing his feet to slow.

She spun about with a squeak, a hand flying to her heart. The other clutched a thick iron key. "Mr. Lockwood!" Her eyes, though wide, were also bright with unshed tears. "What on earth are you doing here?"

He held up his hands. "I'm so sorry to have frightened you. I was upstairs, making arrangements for tomorrow's tour, when I caught sight of your arrival." He drew close. "What can be so wrong that you're spending Christmas Eve here? What with the heat dialed to its lowest setting, you'll be able to see your breath by midnight." The reading room possessed a beautiful vaulted ceiling, but not one designed to conserve heat. Earlier, when they'd left, a chill had already hung in the air.

"There's a fireplace. I thought..." A tear slipped down her cheek.

"Evie?" He chanced to use her given name and held out a hand. "What's wrong?"

She sniffled, then gave a shaky laugh. "Perhaps it's a

sign." Batting away his hand, she stepped closer and dropped her forehead to his chest. The feather of her hat brushed across his cheek. "It's my father. Tonight, he announced his intention to return to a life among the clouds."

Gently, he wrapped his arms about her, gathering her wool-encased form tight against his chest. "But the lesion. Haven't the doctors—"

"Forbidden him from direct sunlight? Yes, of course. But he's never been one to take orders." She huffed into his chest, then started to pull away. "Japan. He's leaving in three days for Japan. At his age... with his condition..." Tears began to brim in her eyes. "He might float away, never to return."

Yet she was here. Why?

Why else?

"Determined to find him a cure? Evie, it's—"

"All but impossible. I know. Physicians have been trying for millennia. But anything I can find before his departure, the airship's doctor can ensure he uses. I have to try." She looked up at him. Glanced away. Swallowed.

He knew that look. There was something more she wasn't telling him. "There's more. What is it?"

A long sigh. "Dr. Bracken appeared at my door, freshly pressed and ironed, flowers in hand."

"And what did he have to say?" Ash growled, knowing he'd not like her answer.

"I've no idea. Wipe that pinched expression from your face. You've no reason to be jealous. Not everyone wishes to marry into the gentry." She gave him a sympathetic glance. "Besides, any claim Dr. Bracken had to nobility passed down another bloodline a generation ago."

Evie knew of Ash's distrust of self-indulgent lordlings, knew about Mary's betrayal. How else to explain the means by which a gardener's son ended up at university? For she too had a dark moment in her past. The death of her fiancé had left her adrift until she found an anchor at Girton College in the form of medieval studies.

"I handled the situation in the most diabolical manner." An evil glint stole into her eyes, and the corners of her mouth curved. "You'll approve. I informed my sister of my plans, then abandoned him to Papa and her six sugar-fueled and over-tired children."

Given Bracken was not a man to be trusted, Ash wasn't entirely satisfied. He wouldn't be, not until *his* ring was on her finger. A symbol for all the world to see. Still, almost against his will, a smile tugged at his lips. "And will they muss up the knife pleats of his trousers?" For a scientist, the man was unusually concerned about his personal appearance.

"If my sister permits their sticky fingers anywhere near them? Most certainly." Evie took a deep breath and waved the iron key. "Enough unpleasantness. We received a donation from a gentleman whose grandfather collected old, rare and unusual medical tomes. Anatomy. Physiology. Written expositions detailing surgical techniques. But, for our purposes, herbals and various pharmacopeia. Several crates full. The donor even promised there was an illuminated manuscript from the 14th century. I meant to tell you, earlier, but was distracted by a certain kiss."

Her teeth caught upon her lip, a motion that shot heat straight to his groin.

His hands fisted in the rough wool of her coat. His gaze dropped to her mouth. Why couldn't he seem to move his thoughts away from her soft, pink lips? "Let me help." He released her. "If there's a new cure in one of those books, we'll find it. It's an entirely selfish offer," he pressed, determined not to take advantage of the situation. "If we find one, not only do we cure your father, we validate the entirety of our project, ensuring we win the committee's approval."

"All true." She looked up at him through her eyelashes. "Though I was hoping you might possess a more *intimate* reason for wishing to remain at my side."

"There's that." He swallowed. Hard.

"That conflicted, hungry expression." She turned away, fitting the key to the lock. "It's only been a few hours, but I've missed it." A teasing glance over her shoulder and a flash in her green eyes singed his every nerve ending. The last of her proper, librarian persona slipped and fell to the ground and was kicked away by her next words. "It draws forth an all but irresistible urge to catch you by the collar and kiss it away. A most inappropriate response, and yet..."

Click. The door swung open, and a cool draft poured out. Winter had crept into the cavernous reading room, but he welcomed the brisk air. Perhaps it would act as antidote to the surging heat that rippled through him.

"Such words…" He followed, stiff with the effort, and attempted a teasing tone. "You would take advantage of an enlightened gentleman who only wishes to offer aid?" If she kept up her comments, steam would soon rise from his skin.

"I would not." A faint blue-white glow intensified as she shook a Lucifer lamp. Her appreciative gaze swept over his form, hot and craving as it lingered upon his bare forearms, upon the cuffs he'd turned up while gardening. It was a measure of how hard he'd fallen for this woman that watching her loose the buttons of her coat was arousing. Over the past two months, he and frustration had become close companions. "We'll work first. Play later."

"Quite the incentive." His heart leapt and lower parts of his anatomy stirred. Perhaps there was hope of sharing a bit more than a few heated kisses this very night, proprieties and traditions be damned. "Can you stop shooting sparks and muster a stern librarian's scowl while you point me at the crate, Miss Brown? Efficiency has become a sudden priority."

"Evie," she said, moving closer to latch the door behind him. "Given our scandalous seclusion in the library after hours, and," she rose on tiptoes to press a quick kiss to his lips, "our recent, immediate, and highly anticipated intimacies, we ought to call each other by our given names."

A dam broke. Every thought of gentlemanly behavior evaporated like dew on grass struck with the sun's first rays. He wrapped his hands around her waist and lifted her onto a table, sealing his lips to hers before plundering her mouth. She tasted of nutmeg and apples and sweet, luscious woman.

My woman.

He would stop. In a moment. But as he wrestled with the primitive part of his mind for control, her fists clutched at the linen of his shirt and dragged him closer. Urging him between her knees. Who was he to deny such demands?

His hands slid beneath her coat, found the small of her back and pulled her to the edge of the table, cursing the frustrations of padded petticoats and billowing skirts that stopped him from yanking her tight against his aching cock. Tongues tangled, thrust and parried.

Her thighs clenched about his hips. Reason was fast escaping him. A deep need welled upward, a need to pierce the silence of this library where only hushed and reasoned discourse transpired. He cupped her breast, caged as it was behind her corset, and swept his thumb over the tip that lay beneath layers of linen, cotton and fine wool. When she pressed into his palm, he gave the peak a sharp pinch and smiled against her mouth as she gasped, imaging her response if he could only lower his lips to her bare flesh.

Her head fell backward. "Ash," she cried, his name a needy sound as she clawed at his waistband.

Fire erupted over his skin. What would it be like to hear her cry his name, louder, faster, in the heat of passion as he buried himself inside her over and over?

While his fingers teased, while her legs wrapped about the backs of his knees. Her fingers threaded into his hair, as he nibbled at the soft skin beneath her ear, nipping, then—when she gasped—soothing his bite with the flat of his tongue.

He wanted nothing more than to toss up her skirts and take her here, on the altar of a reading room table surrounded by the very books she worshipped. Even now, the sharp edge bit into his thighs, heightening rather than diminishing pleasure. Like a desperate thing, need demanded completion.

But he was a civilized man. She was not yet his. There was a proposal. A ring. A wedding date to set.

"Enough." His word was a harsh whisper. "We have to stop."

Hot and sultry, their panting breaths mingled.

"Blazes," she whispered, fanning her fingers across his jawline, over his beard. Her green eyes stared into his. "You make me lose my head."

"Find it, and be sure," he said, dropping note of warning in his voice. "For you hold my heart."

"Ash..."

"Hush. We'll talk more later. First, we attend to more pressing issues." He kissed her nose. "Can you stand?"

She slid down his length, laughing at his agonized groan, to plant her boots solidly on the floor. "You'll have to do better than that if you wish to weaken my knees." Snagging the rolled cuff of his shirtsleeve, she dragged him behind the desk.

He willed his body to quiet, to calm.

Three days. Her project, a subset of their larger one, deserved every ounce of their attention. He loved watching Evie when she was elbow deep in rare and unique texts, delving in to study the time-honored healing properties of plants that had all but slipped away from modern medicine. And those were books that had been catalogued and shelved. Imagine her delight as she delved through an unknown collection. What hidden gems might they unearth?

Deep within the office space of the library, a chamber forbidden to patrons, rested five crates.

"We open them all." Stress, hope, worry pulled at her voice as her gaze flitted from one wooden box to the next. She tossed aside her hat and coat. "Complete an inventory. If there's anything exceptional, we need to know now. And if there's not..."

Her concern tugged at his heart. Better to channel it into action. To have an answer, one way or the other. Picking up the crowbar, he popped off a lid. "No page left unturned."

Bent over the crates, they began to sort through the manuscripts. The limited space in the room forced them to carry the various books out into the reading room. To help chase away the chill, he lit a small fire. Then confiscated a small tea kettle, two cups and a tin of biscuits from Mr. Davies' office and set it upon the grate to boil. Ash would worry about any resultant grumbling by the head librarian another time.

As time passed, dust swirled in the air and piles grew. One for those texts that expounded upon anatomy and physiology. Another for surgical treatises. And, most importantly, one for those that detailed medicinal cures. As expected, the majority of the books were old, but not exceptionally so. Most had originated from a printing press. Yet—Evie gasped and exclaimed—a precious few were hand-lettered parchment, some containing a scattering of painted illustrations.

"Ash." A reverent whisper slipped from her lips. His name and a sound that sent tremors coursing through his body, but her gaze was not on him. Was it possible to be jealous of a book? "Look."

Seated at a table before the fire, she bent over an illustrated manuscript. Loose strands of honey-brown hair brushed over her cheeks framing its vellum pages. Leaning close, he tucked a few tendrils behind her ear, then let the backs of his fingers brush over the soft edge of her jaw.

The nonsensical words—to his eyes—of Old English lined its pages, but the layout and the illustrations were familiar. "An *illustrated* copy of the Old English Herbal?" If so, The British Library could no longer claim to possess the sole such surviving copy.

"Not exactly. I've studied the original, and this appears to be a partial copy. The handwriting is different, the drawings more basic, less detailed. Several herbs are omitted, about half. But..." With great care, she turned the pages. "Look."

His stomach sank. "Ruined." In the margins of nearly every page, the owner had dared to place his own pen to the parchment.

"Not at all." Her voice was bright. "They're known as glosses. Handwritten notations. Many," she pointed an excited finger, "like this one, provide additional details, explanations not contained within the main body of the text. Each is its own gem." Her face was alight with the possibilities. "Collectively, the insight alone is worthy of its own monograph."

One Evie would no doubt write. He smiled, dropping a hand on her shoulder, swept up in her delight. He'd enjoy introducing her as his wife, medieval scholar.

"And the final third of the manuscript?" Ever so carefully, she turned pages. "The texture of the parchment changes." Her fingertip skimmed over an un-inked margin. "There are no more illustrations, and the handwriting of the main body of text matches the earlier glosses. See? The spacing between the words is altered, leaving little space. Taxing to read, even for the most experienced of eyes."

Ash stared at the strange lettering, struggling to discern the differences. Whenever he looked upon Old English lettering, he felt taunted, as if he ought to be able to read and understand its messages, yet it was another language altogether. "The punctuation marks, such as they appear to be, also change."

"Exactly! Judging from the similarities of handwriting, the author of the glosses has written an entirely new herbal. Moreover, she signed her name!"

"She?" That explained a portion of Evie's delight.

"Rare, but not unheard of, for a woman to put pen to parchment." Evie's finger underscored the phrase within the text. "Brea, scribe of *Hardwicke's Leechbook*."

"Most impressive." And fascinating. As was the way Evie vibrated with energy. But she'd failed to address the question of the evening. "Is there any new information?"

"Some of it echoes *Bald's Leechbook*, a ninth century text, but there are unique combinations of herbs prescribed for a variety of conditions—and a number of plants I've never before seen listed in an herbal." Her face tipped upward, aglow with excitement. "The implications for our project are staggering. And if there's a cure for my father, we'll find it here."

CHAPTER SIX

B REA, SCRIBE OF *HARDWICKE'S LEECHBOOK*.
But was she also the author?
The Old English word could be translated both ways.

Evie's heart pounded. Did she have before her an herbal created and used by a female medieval healer? Could it be? A discovery as rare as flying kraken?

Her hands shook as she turned the fragile pages, comparing the glosses with written passages nearer the end.

Careful documentation would be necessary, but the longer Evie studied the hand-bound manuscript, the more she was convinced that this was an undiscovered work. Rare and expensive, parchment was not to be squandered, but there were a number of clues that this missive wasn't penned by a professional scribe. The handwriting was cramped, the lines didn't quite run parallel and, in places, the ink was smeared. All evidence of a less-practiced hand and perhaps less than ideal working conditions.

"Such a treasure," she murmured, "lurking in a private library when it should have been in a scholar's hands being studied, analyzed. For example, this cure for sudden pustules—" She glanced up, searching for a fountain pen and reaching for the battered notebook that was always near her elbow. "If we include this in our presentation to the committee—"

"Evie." Ash's hand fell atop their project notebook, his calm voice reining in her runaway thoughts. "Three days. You—we—will analyze every single last word in this manuscript, but tonight, pustules and coughs and eye complaints are irrelevant. You need to focus on wensalves."

Wennsealfa. Ointments for tumors.

"You're right." She dropped her hand upon his. Only for a moment, lest another *distraction* occur. Some might label it a personal failing, but there were many wonders to be discovered falling down a rabbit hole. Not that she could allow herself to run after white rabbits tonight. If curiosity beckoned, she would need to resist its siren call. For now.

Heart brimming with hope, she flipped to the beginning of the book. "Front to back then, starting with the glosses, then working through the additional text."

"Linear and logical." He dropped a kiss on the top of

her head, then turned back to the towers of books that had grown atop the reading room tables.

Like shiny baubles, Brea's notations on various conditions beckoned, but she resisted her inner magpie and pressed onward. As she sank deeper into her work, time hung in a strange, suspended manner, neither marching forward, nor standing still. She fell into a rhythm where only *wennsealfa* recipes pierced her consciousness. Most were familiar and unaltered, with only a few comments penned by the manuscript's original owner. Nothing earth-shattering, but nonetheless significant. She dutifully took notes recording any adjustments.

As if by magic, a cup of tea and a plate of shortbread appeared upon the table. Her stomach growled. Welcome sustenance.

"Thank you," she said.

Ash left her to her work, turning his attention back to an enormous herbarium with pressed and dried plants mounted upon its pages, examining each with utter and complete concentration. But instead of following his example, Evie indulged herself by stealing a long glance at him while she sipped her tea. Later, when there was time to mount a full and detailed exploration of all his fascinating hard and angular parts, she'd demonstrate her full appreciation for the warm fire, tea and biscuits.

She, a city dweller, had never thought to find herself falling for a botanist, for a man who spent a good part of each day digging in soil and tending to plants. Though Oxford called to her mind, London anchored her heart.

This romance, one snarled by conflicting desires and hopes, had all begun with the hunt for a flower. *Amati-flora*, a name comprised of two Latin roots. *Amat*, love. *Flora*, flower.

Mr. Thistleton, head botanist, had assigned one Mr. Lockwood, a man with an interest in medicinal plants, while Mr. Davies assigned one Miss Brown, a librarian with an academic specialty in ancient texts.

Evie would never forget the first time she'd laid eyes upon Ash.

Curious to visit the rooftop greenhouse—glimpses of which one could catch from the street when the great squares of glass braced by a skeleton of iron glinted and gleamed in the sunlight—Evie had taken it upon herself to initiate introductions.

That rare, sunny, fall day, she'd climbed the stairs to the rooftop, pushed at a door left slightly ajar, and stepped into a humid chamber of greenery where the air held more oxygen than did the entirety of Lister Institute. And so, so much light.

Though beautiful, the various libraries she'd haunted with their neatly ordered shelves of books were still and shadowed. Even those so fortunate as to flaunt arched windows throttled any rays of sun that attempted to penetrate thick panes of wavy glass covered by layers of dust and soot. At best, weak patches of light traced a sedate path across quiet carpets and polished wood floors.

But here in the greenhouse, a multitude of windows were clean and clear, permitting the sun to fuel a riot of growth. Table after table held lines of clay pots, each with its own seedling. About the distant edges of the greenhouse, larger plants dominated, turning the space into a forested, tangled wonderland. Vines twisted up trellises. Ferns rose and curved in great arcs. Bushes hinted at wonders behind the screen of their abundant leaves. And potted trees stretched out their branches, several dangling unusual and brightly colored fruit.

A tall, handsome man with a close-cropped beard caught sight of her. Dropping his trowel, he strolled over. "Can I help you, Miss..."

"Miss Brown." She introduced herself, prim and proper, as was expected from a librarian. "I've been asked to liaise with a Mr. Lockwood."

"You found him," he answered, bowing. "How may I be of assistance?"

"I'm the librarian assigned to work with you, to hunt an unusual flower." She waved the memorandum Mr. Davies had left upon her desk.

His fingers—rough and dirty from his work—caught the sheet of paper and tugged it gently from her hand. "Ah, yes." He glanced upward to study the sky, and light glinted off golden highlights in his hair. "Only a few more hours of sun, then—"

"Later, of course," she stammered, bowled over by an inexplicable attraction and an improper need to stare. It was the first time she'd seen a Lister employee without a cravat, without a waistcoat. Moreover, his shirtsleeves had been rolled to his elbows. Dark hairs scattered across his forearms beckoned, begging to be touched. But there was an audience. This was not the place to flirt. "Perhaps this evening we might meet, discuss our approach?"

A gardener or two cast curious glances in their direction, but Mr. Lockwood didn't seem inclined to offer introductions. "A late night," he asked, "heads bent together over books?" The corner of his mouth hitched upward when the thought of working after hours would have made another man frown. Did she dare hope the magnetic pull she felt toward him was returned at full force?

"A scholarly rendezvous. One involving pen, paper and dusty tomes." A careful answer. After all, they'd just met, and she had no interest in scraping her dignity off the ground before making a swift escape. Still, she offered him an encouraging smile, one designed to give an interested man hope. "Unless you have other plans?"

"None that can't wait." His countenance brightened. So the attraction *was* mutual. "Shall we say six this evening?"

That night—with a wink—he'd passed her a branch of flowering honeysuckle to enliven the library desk. Smiling, she'd led him up the stairs to the balcony where they'd claimed a study alcove as their own. There, over dry herbals and the space of several meetings, their whispered words had often taken on a personal bent. Soon, she'd begun to entertain a fantasy of coaxing Mr. Lockwood deep into the stacks where he might forget to mind his manners.

Mission accomplished.

Evie blinked and found herself back in the library, warm beside a fire, and Ash's steady gaze upon her. If she crooked her finger, would he come running? Most definitely. But, she reminded herself, three days. And, of course, there was the matter of the letter. A sinking feeling overtook her stomach, as if someone had poked a tiny hole in her balloon, initiating a slow leak of the aether that kept her afloat.

She gave Ash a soft smile, then turned her gaze back upon the parchment before her. He deserved to know. She'd tell him. Later. For a glance at the clock had informed her that the evening—Christmas Eve, no less—was wasting.

Impulse made Evie flip to the final section of the book, to the section penned entirely in Brea's hand. If anything unique was to be discovered, it would be upon these coarser sheets of vellum. Here all Latin and Greek words fell away, leaving nothing but Old English.

She dove deeply into the text where an overwhelming abundance of commentary and new formulae beckoned like shiny lures. But tonight there was only one ailment under consideration: *Wennsealfa*.

Turning a page, she forced herself to focus.

Flip. Flip. Flip.

As the end of the manuscript drew close, her heart sank, her shoulders slumped. Even the bioluminescent lamp seemed to give up hope, its blue-white light fading as the hour grew late. If there was a cure to be found for his carcinoma, it wasn't within this library. When dawn arrived, she would go home empty-handed and paste a smile upon her face. For her nephews and her sister—for Papa, she would do her best to celebrate the holiday with cheer.

Flip.

Misteltán. Mistletoe.

The word caught her eye. A plant of contention between her two suitors. Not that there was any competition. For all of Dr. Bracken's physical appeal, she was left with the distinct impression that something was rotten at his core. That his touch might send a slithering coldness across her skin. A certain botanist, however, had only to glance in her direction and the temperature in the room began to rise. His slightest touch provoking an escalating spiral toward spontaneous combustion.

She bent closer.

Curious. Did it say— Evie gave the Lucifer lamp a shake.

A cure from the sacred trees.

Misteltán. Mistletoe. *Āc.* Oak. *Eow.* Yew. *Ellæn.* Elder.

"Ash?" Her voice shook. "I've found something."

"What is it?" Ash leapt to his feet and hurried to her side, staring at the manuscript, at the letters that marched in a row above her fingertip. They formed words, but not ones he could read. Those same words wrapped around a crude diagram inked onto the page. "You'll need to translate."

"A wen-salve," she whispered. "Involving ingredients from three of the trees the Druids considered sacred. Mistletoe from an oak tree. Yew bark. And elderberries." Briefly, she pressed her palms to her eyes, then stared down again at the manuscript, shaking her head. "I'm afraid to believe my eyes."

The base of his neck tingled. Such was a combination they'd yet to encounter. "The mistletoe ointment worked for a time, did it not?"

"It did, but I've no idea of that plant's origin. And this prescription isn't exactly a salve. It's a fluid. Brea instructs a healer to 'drive it deep into the lesion using the sharp tips of needles that it might reach the source' after which a compress soaked in the liquid is to be applied to the tumor. The treatment is to be repeated daily until the lesion is eradicated."

"Ouch." Daily use? Ash winced as he eyed the ink drawing of a wooden shaft into which some ten needles had been embedded. A casual onlooker could not be faulted in thinking it a medieval torture device.

"It rather appears a primitive attempt to perform a subcutaneous injection," she said. "Much more efficient to use a hypodermic syringe to deliver the serum."

"If not less painful." Ash searched his memory. "Three ingredients. Easy enough." *Viscum album, Taxus baccata*, and *Sambucus nigra*. His mind leapt to the sources he had immediately on hand. "We have both potted yew and elder bushes, one still producing berries. And this time of year? It grows late, but mistletoe is available on nearly every street corner." He'd retrieve his coat, dash out, return with a bunch and—

"No." She dropped a hand on his arm. "We'd have no idea of its origin. Better to collect it fresh."

Well, that complicated things, but only slightly. For Evie, he'd venture into a park at night to climb a tree. "Mistletoe grows in Hyde Park." It was near enough. "I've seen it in a lime tree or two—"

"No." She shook her head. "Oak." A certain stubbornness settled over her face as she tapped the page. "This recipe calls for leaves of mistletoe found growing in an oak tree. Crushed and steeped for a day. It's then to be mixed with yew bark—dried and ground into a powder— and crushed elderberries. Here, I'll copy it out." She snatched up a fountain pen and translated the ancient text into modern English.

They had a problem, not with the last two ingredients for they were close at hand, but with the first. Ash dragged a palm down the side of his face. "Evie, mistletoe rarely grows in an oak tree, and the only one I know of is The Druid Oak." His voice trailed off. Not because it was sacrilegious to consider a cure based on an ancient tradition rooted in the Celtic past, but because of the creature.

His lady intended to send him into battle. Not at all a romantic endeavor.

"Exactly." She set aside the pen. "An English oak in

Hyde Park, one guarded by a horrible monster." Amused, she hooked two of her fingers, lifted them and made a chattering sound. "Mengri, clockwork attack squirrel. With beady eyes and long, sharp teeth, he scurries about the branches, chattering and screeching his warnings. Rumor holds that the gypsies possess the windup key, though no one has any evidence as to who its creator might be."

"It's not a rumor or a laughing matter. Haven't you seen the contraption?" Ash threw his hands up. "People pitch peanuts at the thing just to watch it rip through the shells."

"Do they?" She sobered, frowning. "I can't recall the last time I visited the park. I know it's a lot to ask. It's dark, cold, and there's the threat of snow hanging in the air. But perhaps at such a late hour on the eve of a holiday, the creature's clockwork spring will have run down?"

A sound hypothesis, but he very much doubted it. Still there might be something to the healer's insistence that the mistletoe be a plant that grew upon an oak tree.

To the druids, the tree was sacred and the plant a mystery. Suspended between the heavens and the ground, it possessed no roots. Modern botanical studies had revealed the hemiparasitic plant instead possessed haustorium, structures that would grow into its host tree, thus drawing into itself water and nutrients. Different trees produced different nutrients. So perhaps there was something important about the composition of nutrients that the plant removed from an oak tree.

He contemplated his leather boots. Should the squirrel attack, a swift kick ought to knock the contraption away. The perils he was willing to face for Evie knew no bounds. "Grab your coat." With her father's imminent departure, the one resource they couldn't access was time. If there was something special about the plant's growth on oak, then oak it must be. "That mistletoe plant is out on a branch some thirty feet in the air. I'll need a climbing rope. There ought to be one in storage."

Excitement illuminated her face. Leaping to her feet, she launched herself at him, taking flight to throw her arms about his neck. "Thank you!"

Skirts swirled about his legs, silky hair brushed his chin and her soft breasts crushed against his chest. She was far too tempting. Hands upon her corseted waist, he dropped her backward onto her heels. "If you wish to present your father with an ointment as soon as possible, we should go now. But it's near to midnight."

She shook her head. "Is that a problem?"

"Only if you mind returning by way of the service entrance. The entryway passes the morgue." Where Dr. Wilson's remains must lie. Though he left those last words unspoken, she shuddered beneath his palms. "Lister wished to allow the guards to spend the holiday with their families. Well, all but one."

"Which is as it should be." Frowning, she glanced over her shoulder. "We'll go, but what of the books? We can't leave them in such a disarray. Mr. Davies would have my head."

"Plenty of time to set them to rights later, while the mistletoe steeps. Grab your hat and coat." The quick kiss he dropped on her lips brought back her smile. "We've a quest to undertake."

He pulled her from the library, only releasing her hand that she might turn the iron key in its lock, then led her up the stairs.

Minutes later, having quickly retrieved his outerwear, they stood before the botany department's storage room. Climbing a tree, an activity not generally pursued within the city, was a fairly simple task. A thick rope ought to be sufficient equipment.

"Pliny the Elder mentions a golden scythe was used to cut down mistletoe whilst wearing white vestments." A certain lightness lifted Evie's voice and there was a twinkle in her eyes as she glanced about the room.

"I'm afraid we've no white druid robes on hand." He located a hand scythe and passed it to her. "And mere steel will have to do."

"Close enough." She sliced it through the air. "A deterrent should any pickpockets approach. What with that rope wound across your shoulder," Evie slanted him a sideways look and tossed his red muffler over her shoulder before striding off down the hallway, weapon raised, "we don't look like anyone I'd care to meet on a dark night in a park."

Such was a side of Miss Brown—the spirited, enterprising woman who let nothing stop her—that sometimes overtook and subsumed the prim and proper librarian she presented to the world. Both equally enticing aspects of her character.

Grinning, he followed. Prepared to battle a mechanical squirrel to win his lady love.

HE'D MISSED her by minutes.

The library was deserted, but the teapot was still warm. A Lucifer lamp flickered, and a fire burned low in the grate. A half-eaten biscuit rested on a plate. An abandoned fountain pen leaked ink onto a notebook page.

Bracken frowned.

Never before had Miss Brown revealed an inclination toward chaos. Tidy and meticulous with her grooming, her words and her work, the disarray spread before him spoke of a hastily abandoned project but gave no indication of where she might have gone. Not that it mattered. She would be back to set things straight, lest her supervisor discover her late-night foolishness.

There would be time to break any bad habits later.

Bracken stepped back, surveying the scene before him. It appeared Miss Brown had spent a cozy evening before the fireplace, reading an ancient manuscript while taking notes and sipping tea. Given the disordered piles of moldering, old books stacked upon nearby tables, she'd gone to some length to locate that singular, leather-bound volume.

Keen to assess its value, he opened the cover and flipped through a few pages. And rolled his eyes. Old English. What possible use were such texts in a facility dedicated to advancing the medical sciences?

Closing the book, he shoved it aside, turning his attention to a familiar brown notebook, curious as to what brought her to the Lister Institute on Christmas Eve. He'd seen Miss Brown and Lockwood passing it back and forth between them, conferring over its contents, scribbling notes, and generally acting as if it was a classified document.

A tryst with the gardener would explain her absence.

Steam gathered beneath his collar. He'd give her a chance to explain her whereabouts. Perhaps her actions had an innocent explanation. For her sake, he dearly hoped so.

Nonetheless, such forays must stop. No wife of his would ever be caught traversing the streets of London alone in the dead of night.

Not that her father had seemed particularly receptive to the idea of marrying off his daughter to prevent such antics.

"The choice is hers." Her sire's voice had been gruff, rather than gracious.

Not even the sight of an heirloom ring or the recitation of a generous marriage settlement inclined the man toward more solicitous behavior. At least, given the glimpse Bracken caught of a lesion beneath the old gasbag's mask, there was little chance his soon-to-be father-in-law would exert a long-term influence upon his daughter. A happy thought.

In a room conjured by an air bandit's drunken fantasy, Bracken had prepared to press his suit, but their conversation was interrupted by the onslaught of far too many boys—all over-tired, loud and sticky. In hopes of speaking with Miss Brown herself, he'd allowed the collective lot to drag him upstairs to the parlor for the annual lighting of the Yule log, a quaint pagan tradition rarely observed in more enlightened communities.

While there had at least been a tree, Miss Brown herself was pointedly absent.

"A stomach complaint," her sister apologized.

"We're not supposed to lie, Mama," one of the older boys piped up, turning to Bracken. "I saw her leave from the window."

"Something about a book," another boy added.

"Now, now," the child's mother chided, flushed with embarrassment. "Our guest doesn't need to be told such things."

But he did. A gentleman had a right to know every-thing about the woman he planned to marry, and this was a facet of her character which required closer examina-tion. Leaving the house at night unattended was improper at best. A wife ought not exhibit such indepen-dence. Was it a trait that could be corrected? Or would he need to resort to stronger actions such as those which had been applied to the problem of Dr. Wilson?

Taking his leave, he'd returned to the Lister Institute. He and Miss Brown needed to have a private conversation about their future.

While he waited, he'd take the opportunity to inspect the contents of this notebook. Miss Brown and Lockwood were up to something. And he'd know precisely what before her return.

CHAPTER SEVEN

T HE WIND HAD PICKED UP since she'd arrived
at Lister, and the cold had acquired a sharp
bite, creeping beneath the cuffs of her sleeves
and slipping around the hem of her skirts to nip at wrists
and ankles. But the bright red muffler Ash had wound
about her neck kept her warm in more ways than one. As
did the excitement of a late-night excursion.

More than one person's head had turned, confusion
and curiosity at the sickle in her hand making them blink
and question their eyesight. She'd tipped her head up to
catch Ash's gaze and smiled, though it was very unlady-
like to enjoy such appreciative stares that set her pulse
fluttering.

They turned a corner, walking into a headwind that
plucked and tore at her hat, ripping it free from its hat
pin and sending it skittering down the street.

"Oh!" she cried.

Ash lunged on her behalf but was too late. The hat landed in a gutter. "I'm sorry."

"Never mind." She slid her arm through his. She refused to mourn its loss. "Casualties are to be expected during important expeditions. It'll feel more like an adventure with the wind blowing through my hair." A few locks had torn loose, though not enough to diminish any appearance of respectability.

He lifted an eyebrow. "So long as it's the only casualty."

"It's but a clockwork squirrel." Yet her words held a forced confidence, and the look that crossed Ash's face let doubt slip into her question. "How menacing can it be?"

"Wait until you see the contraption."

"Is it known to attack people?" A frisson of unease wound itself about her chest, ready to squeeze tight.

His lips twisted. "Not yet."

She frowned. "If the gypsies set the contraption to guard the tree, might they know something of the mistletoe's healing properties that we do not?"

"Entirely possible," Ash replied. "Though the old woman, the gypsy healer Nadya who pointed us at the *amatiflora*, has disappeared. Her people will only say she's 'gone traveling'. Rather unfortunate. Our project could benefit from her expertise."

"Well," Evie processed this new information, "I'll not have you take any unnecessary risks."

If they needed to delay their strange harvest, they could return tomorrow with assistance. What mattered most was the safety of the man at her side who had stolen her heart. It was a rare man who would be willing to scale an oak tree on Christmas Eve as the midnight hour approached, all to chase down a rare ingredient suggested by an unknown healer from a tradition that lay centuries in the past.

Perhaps even longer. Druids had passed along their knowledge via an oral tradition, and only a few Romans had recorded their practices—and that with an outsider's eye. Her mind drifted back to Brea's proposed treatment involving three of the sacred trees. The druids believed the oak tree sacred and used mistletoe to concoct an elixir —other ingredients unknown—that was thought to be a cure-all. Was it possible they'd stumbled onto some ancient wisdom? Aether, she hoped so. On its own, mistletoe could be poisonous if consumed in large enough quantities. But the ancient cure was only for topical usage.

Her mood deflated at the thought of Papa floating away, perhaps never to return. During her childhood, every time he left on a long voyage, he'd made much of his last days on shore, dragging her, her sister and her mum about London, splurging on treats such as hair ribbons, new shoes, and ices at Gunther's. Not until she was older had she realized why there was such sadness in her mother's eyes whenever an airship was set to lift away.

Yet Papa's floating career had lifted them within society, providing their family with all the comforts they could want, save a cure for the lesion upon his face. If her years at Girton College, if her knowledge of Old English could save him, there was little she wouldn't do to place this new chance for a cure in his hands.

They hurried across a street, and the tops of Hyde Park's trees came into view. Almost there. They weaved through a dwindling straggle of shoppers, past coster-mongers hawking the last of their wares, hoping to sell a few more meat pies, holly wreaths, oranges—

"Nuts!" A young man with a tray suspended from his neck shouted. "Roasted chestnuts!"

She tugged them to a halt. "Wait." Evie pulled off her mitten and shoved her hand beneath her coat. Working the knot of her purse, she pulled out a coin and dropped it into his waiting palm.

Ash's eyebrows rose. "For the—er—squirrel?"

If the peddler thought it odd that a young couple proposed to feed the city's wildlife as the hour approached midnight, he gave no indication as he shoved a paper bag of hot chestnuts into her hands.

"Potential ammunition to distract the creature. Besides, they smell so good. Mmm." She breathed in the nutty scent, then plucked one free and offered it to Ash. "A shame to waste them *all* on a creature that doesn't possess taste buds."

His lips parted, then caught at her fingers as she slipped the chestnut into his mouth, giving their tips a quick nip. A rush of heat rippled over her. Blazes, but he was good with his mouth. The moment they were back inside Lister, she intended to invite another one of his bone-melting kisses.

Ash grinned, as if reading her mind, but gave none of his own thoughts away with his reply. "I thought you were operating under the assumption that the clockwork squirrel, having wound down on a holiday that few would observe with a jaunt into the park, would be frozen motionless?"

"And rendered harmless," she maintained. "After all, who would be out this night tending such a creature?"

"Have you not heard that the Queen granted a small band of Romanichal gypsies permission to spend the winter in Kensington Gardens?"

"She did?"

He nodded. "In remembrance of the losses they suffered and to thank them for disclosing the nature and location of the *amatiflora*."

"That was kind." It did, however, alter her perception of the likelihood of encountering an active clockwork contraption, a particularly well-developed talent within the gypsy community. If designed and built by the skilled Roma, they would do well to not underestimate the creature's potential abilities. She tightened her grip upon both the scythe and the sack of chestnuts. "If Mengri is on duty, I'll do my best to keep him occupied."

A hush fell over them as they crossed into the park and moved away from street traffic. Only a few people wandered in the park at this hour, their forms distant—

and nonthreatening—shadows. Not that it would do to drop her guard.

Gravel crunched beneath their boots. Wind whistled through bare branches. Birds rustled inside trimmed shrubbery. Wildness, carefully cultivated and controlled.

A row of lampposts cast alternating patterns of light and dark as they followed the walkway leading to The Druid Oak. At last it rose before them, branches reaching into the midnight sky where a few leaves still clung hero-ically. At its base, peanut shells littered the ground, tossed there by those who'd visited the tree in search of an afternoon's diversion.

She stepped closer. A meshwork of tiny claw marks scarred the bark. Her stomach tightened. Proof that something with sharp toe-tips did indeed frequent this trunk. But why set a guard upon the tree? Who else in London would go through the trouble of harvesting mistletoe from an oak tree when so many bundles were easily purchased in shops or readily harvested from more accessible apple trees?

"Mengri?" She clicked her tongue and tossed a chestnut into the branches. *Thud.* It bounced off a limb and dropped to the ground. "Are you there?" She threw another. *Thunk.* And another. *Thwack.* "See? No sharp-toothed clockwork creature to speak of." The knot loos-ened in her stomach. Perhaps she'd been right. Its mecha-nisms had wound down, though her supposition was based on no more than a hunch and a prayer. Good. She hoped damp had seeped into the squirrel's joints and frozen them solid.

"LET'S HOPE SO." Ash shrugged off his coiled rope, unhooked a bioluminescent torch and shook it to life. He cast its light into the branches.

Over thirty feet above them, suspended from a branch, hung a tangled ball of forked stems bearing leaves and white berries. Out of reach for most. Precious few Londoners had grown up in the countryside, and far fewer made a habit of climbing tall trees, especially into adulthood. None but adventurers, scientists and gardeners who trimmed trees for a landowner. A long ladder and a pole saw might manage it, but such maneuvering would be difficult in the dark of night. Climbing was quicker and easier.

"There," he pointed. "Do you see it?"

Arms crossed and rubbing her shoulders against the rising cold, Evie tipped her head back. "I do."

Aether, he loved seeing his scarf wrapped about her neck. The warm, protective feeling it engendered went beyond wanting to peel it away, to kiss the soft skin of her neck, though it certainly included such thoughts.

The sooner they retrieved the mistletoe, the sooner they could return to Lister... and visit his greenhouse where it was warm, snug and private. Where he might lead her down a garden path in hopes of more than a few kisses.

"You want the whole thing?" He handed Evie the torch. The plant looked to have about three years of growth. If he gathered most, but not quite all, it would regenerate.

She nodded. "I'd rather not return."

A sentiment with which he agreed.

Wrapping the rope into a throwing bundle, Ash tossed the mass high into the air, over the second lowest branch some fifteen feet from the ground. He gave the climbing rope a sharp tug, pulling it taut into the crux between branch and trunk and tied it about his waist. He hooked the hand scythe to his belt, checked his harness, then clipped and knotted it to a second rope. Wrapping his fists about the rope, he gave a great yank and planted the soles of his boots against the bark. Hand over hand, he began to walk up the trunk of the tree.

Below, Evie circled about the great oak's base, her head cocked, listening for trouble.

"Do we have a problem?" he called.

"For a moment I thought I heard—"

Clack.

"That!" she called. "Did you—"

Clack. Clack.

"Yes." He pulled harder and walked faster.

Clack. Clack. Clack.

"Ash!" Evie pointed the blue-white light of the torch into the branches. "It's above you!"

He saw the red eyes first. Two tiny glowing embers set in a silver face topped by two wire-tufted ears. Its teeth weren't long, but they did look sharp. The bioluminescent light highlighted teethed-gears, pistoned legs, and a bottle-brush wire tail. Its maker, possessed of an odd humor, had fitted the clockwork creature with a tiny waistcoat, complete with miniature brass buttons. Added entertainment for those who made the pilgrimage to visit the tree?

"I see him." Tugging on the rope, he advanced two steps.

Scratch. Scrabble. Scratch. On tiny needle toes, it scrambled off the branch and spiraled around the trunk, drawing eye level. Mengri opened his glinting metal mouth and began to make a strange, chiding noise that scraped along Ash's nerves. "*Screech. Chit. Chit. Chit.*"

"That's a warning," Evie called. "Be careful."

An annoying contraption. He resumed his assent. Once he reached a branch, he could swipe at the creature with the sickle, knock loose a few springs. How sturdy could it be?

Over and over the clockwork squirrel screamed at him. *Screech. Chit. Chit. Chit. Screech. Chit. Chit. Chit.*

It bunched up its jointed, metal body and sprang from the trunk, landing on Ash's boot. The thick leather protected his ankles from Mengri's sharp, needle-like toes, but this was no mere toy. Ash tried to kick it free, but the squirrel held tight, rearing back to sink its incisors through the wool of Ash's trousers and deep into the skin of his leg.

"Aaarrrh!" Ash dropped backward as pain loosened his grip on the rope.

The squirrel leapt away. *Screech. Chit. Chit. Chit.*

"Ash! Are you all right?"

Not exactly. "I'm fine," he called, yanking harder, climbing faster, wanting to reach that first branch before the next attack.

"Mengri!" Evie called from beneath. *Thunk.* A chestnut hurled past into the branches.

But the squirrel was not deterred. Not in the least. It attacked again, landing on Ash's shoulder and sinking its teeth into his ear. "Ow!" Blood trickled down the side of his neck. He swatted the creature away. But it didn't go far. It leapt onto Ash's head. Sharp pinpricks of pain dug into his scalp.

Thunk. Thunk. Chestnuts, now defensive missiles, flew past. But Evie's aim was awful and the squirrel fast.

Screech. Chit. Chit. Chit. The creature leapt away.

Ash reached his branch and pulled himself onto it. Sitting some fifteen feet in the air, he tied a security line to another branch above his head. Falling from this height was unlikely to kill him, but it would do significant damage. He glanced upward at the ball of mistletoe. Taking a header from thirty feet would, however, ensure his death.

"He." *Thunk.* "Won't." *Thunk.* "Quit!" *Thunk.*

Screech. Chit. Chit. Chit. Overhead, Mengri scurried

along the branch and sank his gleaming teeth into Ash's hand.

Cursing, he yanked his arm away, teetering for a moment upon the thick limb.

Determined. Destructive. And, should Ash lose his grip, quite possibly deadly.

The higher he climbed, the narrower the branches would become, and Ash could not afford to battle a mechanical squirrel the whole way up.

He unhooked the scythe and beckoned Mengri closer, prepared to slash at the clockwork demon. "Come here closer, rodent. I'd like nothing more at this moment than to remove your head, you evil little creature."

Ash swung the scythe, but missed.

Mengri vaulted back to the trunk, screeching, a horrible, high-pitched tone. Soon Ash's eardrums would begin to bleed.

"Come down!" Evie called. "We'll contact the botany department at Kew Gardens. They must know of another tree."

But they would be closed tomorrow. By the time another oak tree hosting mistletoe was located, her father would have floated away.

"I've." *Slash.* "Almost." *Slash.* "Got him."

"Best attempt yet," a voice spoke from below. A gypsy man leaned casually against a nearby lamp post. A peddler returning to his Kensington camp, unsold ivy wreaths dangling from a stick over his shoulder. "You seem rather set on stealing my mistletoe."

LEASH A MINK! Evie nearly jumped out of her skin. She'd been far too focused on hitting that miserable clockwork beast and not minding the shadows that skulked through the dark of night. Her heart pounded as she stared at one that had emerged to materialize in a pool of lamplight beside her.

"Yours?" Evie cried. "How can it be yours?"

"Because I planted it, of course." The gypsy man squinted upward. "Admittedly, I planted them for an old healer woman. But it's hard to get mistletoe to take to an oak tree. Five years ago, I cut more than fifty of those sticky seeds into its bark, and only one grew. So, yes. Mine."

Screech. Chit. Chit. Chit.

"Make it stop!" Evie pitched more chestnuts at the beast. She was fast running out, but anger mixed with worry, and she couldn't bring herself to stop.

The gypsy clicked his tongue. "A shameful waste."

"Excuse me!" Ash yelled down. "Is there an off switch?"

Evie shot the gypsy a hard look, but he only lifted a shoulder. "Of a sort. For a price."

"How much?" she demanded, then pitched another chestnut.

Crunch! Ash's booted toe connected with the clock-work squirrel, knocking it to the ground.

As it sat amidst the litter of nuts and shells, Evie

ripped off her coat and lunged, flinging the heavy fabric at the squirrel. A failed attempt at netting the creature. Even now it spiraled back up the oak tree, chattering its irritation.

The gypsy man only laughed. "Make me an offer," he countered.

"A shilling," she answered without the slightest flinch. Some might find it tough to focus on bartering with shouts raining down as the clockwork squirrel attacked Ash again. But how many times had she negotiated peace terms for her nephews with all of them screaming at once? Still, this needed to be quick, and there was no time for the finer points of deliberation. She'd pay any price to keep Ash safe. The gypsy's attack squirrel could do very real harm.

The gypsy grinned. "Twenty pounds."

"What!"

He lifted his chin. "That oak mistletoe is valuable. I'm not *giving* it away."

She altered her approach. "How much to stop the squirrel while we discuss the plant's value?"

"One pound."

Evie yanked off her mitten and dug into her purse to produce a sovereign. She held it between her fingers. "Make it stop."

Setting aside his wreaths, the man pulled a tin whistle from his pocket, laid his fingers atop the holes, then gave it a blow. Its pitch was almost as piercing as the squirrel's screams. "*Rúkkersaméngri! 'Chavaia!* Stop."

Ah, so that was where the creature's name originated.

The clockwork beast froze upon the outstretched branch, its eyes blinking in the dark night.

Ash tugged free his glove, sucked blood from a wound on his hand, then stood, as if to climb once more.

"No climbing up," the gypsy yelled. "Only down. She has only paid for a safe retreat." He turned a mischievous look in Evie's direction. "Unless you wish to purchase the mistletoe?"

"I'll give you two pounds more."

He grinned, clearly enjoying their exchange. "No. Why do you want my mistletoe so badly? No need to cut it down to steal a kiss beneath it."

"There's a medicine I wish to make."

His eyes lit with interest. "Ah, you know something of the secrets of the oak tree. Not so many do. Even I was not made privy to the specifics of its healing powers, though Nadya often crafted it into a drink for childless couples."

Evie crossed her arms and set her mouth into a stubborn line. She said nothing. To agree would only drive the price up.

"That crazy man must love you very much, to take on my *Rúkkersaméngri.*" The gypsy lifted an eyebrow, letting his gaze rake down her form. "But you're young. Too soon for fertility problems. The problem probably lies with him. Choose another man."

"It's not for us. Me." Her face flushed. "Three pounds."

The gypsy laughed. "Ten."

Evie unclipped her purse from the chain about her waist. "Four. It's all I have."

"Mmm." The man looked pained at the choices she presented. He tapped his fingers against the tin whistle. What mattered more, the plant or her money? "Only if you leave the roots. It grows back, but slowly. Someday, the healer might return and have questions for me."

"Fair enough. Provided you keep that clockwork squirrel sitting still while he harvests the plant."

"Done." A grin split his face. "*Rúkkersaméngri!*" He blew into the whistle. "*Av akai!* Come here."

The mechanical creature scurried down the trunk and across the ground, scrambling up the gypsy's coat to perch upon his shoulder. The tiny waistcoat the squirrel wore would have made it look harmless, save for the glowing red eyes and the blood dripping from its incisors.

"There, no more worries." He turned and yelled into the tree. "Climb. The mistletoe is now yours, but leave the roots. I'll stay, watch, and keep your woman company. With all that loose, windblown hair of hers, I might need to discourage other interested parties." He winked and dropped his voice. "I'm warm too, if you'd like to step closer?"

Not liking the speculative look in his eyes, she tossed him the purse from a distance. "I'm warm enough." She wasn't, but she'd manage. To distract him, she nodded to the clockwork creature. "His name?"

"*Rúkkersaméngri,*" he said. "Squirrel in Romani. But

he also answers to English if you play the right notes. I'm quite proud of him. Your man is the first to present my creature with a right proper battle." He scooped up her coat and held it out to her on a hooked finger. "Most foppish gentlemen turn tail and run after the first tiny nip."

Eyes narrowed and doing her best not to shiver from the cold, she snatched it from his hands and pulled it on. "Lovely. I suppose you mean that as a compliment."

"I do. Better a man with a spine than one without." He winked. "I'd say the same of a woman. What did you say your name was?"

"I didn't." A firm answer, if not quite a polite one.

She turned away to keep an eye on Ash, but the gypsy's flattery had found its mark. A faint smile crept onto her face.

WITH THE MANIC SQUIRREL REMOVED, Ash finally ascended to the top branches of the oak some thirty feet off the ground. Not as quickly as he might have, were he not—with every stop to throw his climbing rope higher—hurling barbed glares at the much-amused gypsy man beneath. With Ash's every glance, the man seemed a foot closer to Evie.

The mistletoe belonged to them, but only after Evie was relieved of her entire purse. Ash eyed the clockwork creature as it sat quietly upon the gypsy's shoulder, then worked quickly, reluctantly impressed by the usefulness of the contraption.

With one blast of his tin whistle and a command, the squirrel could become a blur of sharp teeth and claws. An effective, yet not quite deadly, deterrent. As it was, Ash needed several sticking plasters to cover the multitude of tiny gashes carved into his skin.

With the hand sickle, he sliced off all but a few branches of the mistletoe, tying them into bunches and hanging them from his belt. There would be no admiring how the city lay blanketed by dark snow clouds, not with the gypsy making advances.

Ten minutes later, his feet once again touched the ground.

"Thank you!" Evie launched herself at him, pressing a kiss to his cheek.

Pushing the bundle of mistletoe onto one hip, Ash caught her with his arm, pulling her to his side. Bells began to ring, announcing the midnight hour and the arrival of Christmas. A snowflake lazily drifted downward, landing upon the tips of her eyelashes.

Tempted to kiss it away, he was reminded of their audience by an amused half-cough.

The gypsy man's lips twisted as he eyed the bunches —and Ash's future bride. "You're a lucky man."

"I am," Ash replied, eyes narrowed in warning. Their deal was done, and he wished to be on his way without further interference.

"On account of the holidays, your injuries, and your

lovely companion, a gift." The gypsy fussed with bolt on the contraption's side, drawing out a metal bar with braided cotton fabric protruding from one end. "A cribiform wick, designed to register all manner of odors." He drew the soft cotton across Ash's cheek, then Evie's. He replaced the braided string and refastened the bolt back. "Now he has your scent and will, provided the wick remains in place, never attack either of you again." He held the tin whistle out to Evie. "Cover the top hole for 'stop'. The top two holes for 'come'. And the top three for 'attack'."

"And the last three?" she asked, leaning forward to accept the gift.

The gypsy shrugged a shoulder and winked. "Silliness and antics."

Evie rolled her eyes, but pressed fingertips to the top holes and blew. "Come," she ordered the clockwork squirrel.

Ash winced as Mengri leapt from the gypsy's shoulder onto his own.

A gift? More likely a curse.

Then again, if the mistletoe concoction worked, then they might wish to set the clockwork squirrel back on its watch. Not that there would be enough mistletoe growth to guard until late spring at the earliest.

"Ah, he has a favorite," the man laughed. Then, with a tip of his hat, he hoisted his rack of wreaths and strolled away. "Happy Christmas!"

CHAPTER EIGHT

"I'M SO SORRY. I'D NO IDEA a clockwork squirrel could be so very vicious!" Evie side-eyed the motionless contraption. Frowned at the dark stain upon its incisors. Then angled Ash's chin away, directing the fall of lamplight onto his ear. Dried blood trailed down the side of his neck. "Aether, its bite pierced your ear!"

"And other bits, not to mention my pride." He plucked Mengri from his shoulder and stuffed it into his coat pocket. "I may have lost the battle, but your ransom won us the spoils of war." He dipped his head and captured her lips with his.

A celebratory kiss that breathed pure oxygen onto banked coals. She parted her lips to let him slip inside. He groaned, kissing her harder, with a hunger that left her in no doubt that he too had replayed their earlier kiss in his mind and also wanted so, so much more. Flames rose to lick at her body, and she wrapped her arms about his waist, running her hands up his back beneath his coat, over the linen covering strong muscle, higher—

Wet and sticky cloth met her fingertips.

Aghast, she pulled away. "Your shirt is torn! How bad is it?" Circling him, she took in the long slash the mechanical animal's teeth—or claws—had torn in his overcoat with a gasp. "Let's go. These lacerations need to be cleaned."

"In a moment." Ash caught her hand and spun her about, pulling her to his chest. "The pain is manageable. How often will we have a chance like this? Unless, of course, you're cold?"

Snowflakes swirled about as he walked her backward, until she felt the rough bite of bark at her back as he pinned her to the oak tree with his delightfully solid weight. The hunger in his eyes shot a new rush of heat straight to her frozen toes. "Cold?" She stroked the close-cropped beard at the edge of his jaw with her thumb. Not with such a thrilling heat source raising the temperature. "Is it winter?"

His laugh was almost a low growl as he unwound the thick muffler from about her neck, letting it drape about her shoulders. "Hard to say. It feels like midsummer." With one hand he popped free the first button of her coat, then ran a fingertip along the edge of her collar, tracing the pattern of embroidery. "What with vines running rampant, twisting in invitation."

She dropped her head back against the tree trunk.

Cold air nipped at her neck, but it was anticipation that sent a shiver across her skin. "As was intended."

"Good." Warm lips brushed over the soft skin beneath her ear. *Pop.* Another fastening came undone, this time the one that held her collar closed.

"Ash." Her whisper was a plea. She slid her fingers once more beneath his jacket to grip the waistband of his trousers.

His kisses fell along the edge of her jaw, then trailed downward, stopping to nip and suck at the curve of her neck. With each bite, an aching warmth between her legs grew, and only the frosty night air kept her from melting into a puddle at his feet. This was the delicious danger of secluded gardens, a danger that made girls far more innocent than her willing to risk their reputations.

Lips met hers again. A hard kiss, one demanding she answer in kind. She tipped her head back delighting in the rough scrape of bark across her scalp as if she were a dryad, at one with the great tree at her back.

Opening her mouth, she groaned at the warm, slick slide of his tongue over hers. A deep, drugging kiss driving her mad, pushing all awareness from her mind. Save for where their bodies met. Her world reduced to the flick of his tongue, to the crush of her breasts, to the frustration of their hips, separated by an exasperating thickness of wool, cotton and linen. Cloth foiling any hope of further explorations.

Chit. Chit. Chit. A muffled complaint from Mengri emerged from the depths of Ash's pocket.

He tore his mouth away with a curse. "That damn squirrel. It needs to be stuffed away in a locked box." His voice was thick and gruff, and his next words touched a match to the smoldering need his kisses had sparked. "Might I escort you directly to the greenhouse for a tour? We'll set the mistletoe to steep, then I've wonders to show you."

"That confident, are you?" She laughed softly.

His eyes flashed. "Would a man dare to make such midnight promises and fail to deliver?"

She bit her lip, pretending to consider the question. "It *is* Christmas. And I can't help but wonder what you have in mind." Her voice was a husky whisper, for there was little breath left in her lungs. Amidst all those plants in the greenhouse, there would be warmth, privacy, and more than enough oxygen. Plenty to fuel the combustion that threatened between them. She brushed a dusting of snow off his hair. "I'd like nothing better than to pass the small hours beneath the fronds of tropical plants while snow falls upon the glass above us."

As they gathered up the rope and hand sickle to leave the park, Evie sent a silent thank you to Mengri, for sending them on their way.

By the time they crossed back onto city streets, now all but deserted, a fine coat of snow covered the pavement. Ash kept an arm about her waist to protect her from the slippery surface while keeping a careful hand atop the bundle of precious mistletoe tied to his belt.

A faint unease crept up her spine, as they rounded a

corner and approached one of Lister Institute's lesser known entrances. One that led to the morgue. Inside, Dr. Wilson's remains would await a final verdict as to the precise nature of the blast that killed him and injured several others.

Ash stiffened as they approached the door. "The guard is rather more bright-eyed than one might expect for such an hour. Something is afoot."

Ash pressed a hand to the security pad, held still as the pectin coagulator verified his identity. *Click.* A green light flashed, and the door popped open. They started inside.

"Stop, please." The guard turned suspicious eyes upon them, barely giving the mistletoe a glance. "I'll need the lady to verify her authorization as well."

Evie pressed her hand to the pad. The green light flashed.

"Thank you." The guard held out his hand. "I'll also need to see your identification cards."

With the slightest hesitation, Ash produced his identity card. "An unusual request," he commented. "Palm identification is quite rigorous. What's going on?"

The guard recorded Ash's name and time of entry. "Standard procedure for holiday entry." As he handed the card back, the guard lifted an eyebrow. "Any particular reason you ask, Mr. Lockwood?"

"None."

Evie fumbled with the buttons of her coat, slid her hand into her pocket. Was the guard recording names? If so, why? She'd never been told *not* to work after hours, but should Mr. Davies be informed of her unusual late arrival, would he demand an explanation? Remove her from the joint project with Ash? Her corset felt overly tight. *Bells and blazes*, would it jeopardize her offer from Oxford?

Only now did she realize how badly she wished to accept the scholarship. She also wanted this night with Ash. She straightened, putting some starch in her spine. This mistletoe experiment was important. Doubly so. For if it succeeded, it would benefit both her father and others. Her presence was important, as much so as those rare female agents who freely came and went from Lister at all hours. Why not her?

Both men looked to Evie. Unless she wished to turn about and return home, there was no choice but to comply. Cowardice would win her nothing. She must count on Mr. Davies being unable to resist the lure of academic grandeur for the library.

She held out her card.

The guard picked up his pen but hesitated as he wrote down her name. "If you'll wait here a moment, Miss Brown." He did not return her card. Instead, he marched down the hall and rapped upon a closed door.

Evie rose onto her toes and whispered, "What's going on?" The guard conversed with someone inside a room. "Are those interrogation rooms?"

"They are. This is most unusual." Ash gave her hand a quick squeeze, dropping it when a man emerged.

"Mr. Lockwood. Miss Brown. How utterly convenient." The sardonic voice belonged to a dark-haired
gentleman. Not one she recalled ever visiting the library,
but as he knew *her*.

"Have we..." Recognition struck. "You're Mr. Black.
From the... explosion."

He offered her a faint smile, though he looked tired
about the eyes. "Guilty." He waved his hand toward the
room. "I realize the hour is late, but we've been looking
for you."

"Me?" Incredulity made her voice squeak. "Whatever for?"

"We've a few questions concerning Dr. Bracken's
recent behavior."

Dr. Bracken's dramatic cry as he'd rushed to his
colleague's fallen form sprang to mind. She'd chalked it
up to attention-seeking behavior, but if Dr. Wilson's
death had been determined to be foul play and they were
seeking out the chemist... and had linked her name to his.

Her heart pounded. Aether, she'd abandoned her
family with Dr. Bracken upon the doorstep. Holding
flowers. A prospective suitor.

A sick feeling stirred deep in her stomach. They
couldn't possibly think her an accomplice, could they?

"Our relationship is a purely professional one." Evie
found her feet nailed to the floor.

"Yet we've information to the contrary." His voice
was firm, and Mr. Black waved his hand toward the open
door. "If you'll both step inside, have a seat?"

"Do we have a choice?" Ash asked, wary.

"Not really, Mr. Lockwood. Time is of the essence."

ASH EYED the small interrogation room. It didn't look nearly as terrifying as one might expect. An overly bright light hung overhead. There were three chairs. And a wooden table upon which stained papers were stacked. Behind it, chipped teacup at his elbow, sat none other than Lord Thornton.

"Tormenting potential witnesses again, Black?" Lord Thornton asked in a deep booming voice, rising. His face was all sharp angles and planes, softened only by stray curls that twisted at the ends of his dark locks. Not a face that encouraged a person to relax.

"Slipping in through the morgue entrance at the midnight hour, one with a rope slung about his shoulder while the lady carries a hand scythe?" Mr. Black lifted an eyebrow. "They're up to *something*."

Lord Thornton sighed. "And yet you let her keep the weapon."

"They don't look dangerous." Mr. Black tipped his head. "Instead, they've the air of a tryst about them, wouldn't you say?"

Beside him, Evie's face flushed.

Ash did not care for the direction this interview was taking. "We were in Hyde Park," he indicated the bundle of mistletoe that hung at his hip, "collecting mistletoe growing upon an oak tree, a necessary ingredient for a botanical cure."

"Is that—?" Mr. Black leaned forward. His eyebrows drew together as he stared. "It's *Rúkkersaméngri,* the clockwork squirrel from The Druid Oak."

The creature had popped its head out of Ash's pocket. He stuffed it back inside. "The very one."

"Well that explains the state of your face." Mr. Black snorted. "And your need for sticking plaster."

Exasperated, Ash huffed. "Do you require a detailed explanation of our project, or will it suffice to say that I'm a botanist facing a tight timeline and that Miss Brown is a colleague in possession of valuable historic insight?"

Lord Thornton's lips twitched. "As our questions pertain to Dr. Bracken, we'll consider the nature of your nighttime wanderings irrelevant." He pulled out a chair. "Miss Brown. Mr. Lockwood. Please, sit. We'll try to keep this short." His voice held notes of frustration and impatience. "Were it not important, it would not keep me from my wife on such a night."

Evie lowered herself onto the edge of the seat.

"Is this about Dr. Wilson's death?" Ash ignored the earl's invitation. He preferred to remain standing. "It was deliberate then, the explosion?"

Without answering, Mr. Black directed his next statement to Evie. "We're attempting to locate Dr. Bracken. I've information that suggests he is a suitor of yours."

Evie stiffened. "Certainly not."

"Yet I'm told he paid a visit to your home this

evening, flowers in hand, and was welcomed inside where he remained for some time." The agent's eyes never left Evie's face.

Jealousy nipped at Ash's heels, but he bit his tongue. He had no cause. Bracken moved among the gentry and had resources—financial and social—that Ash could never hope to offer her, but Evie had made her preference for him clear. He smirked. It warmed the heart to know the chemist was wanted for questioning in a possible murder case.

Did they think Bracken responsible?

Why else would they go to the trouble of tracking his movements on Christmas Eve?

"I told my sister to tell him I was ill, to turn him away, then I slipped away via the kitchen door." Evie's face burned a furious red. "Dr. Bracken is a colleague who oversteps his bounds, making uninvited and unwelcome advances."

Mr. Black leaned a shoulder against the doorframe. "Ones distasteful enough to send you fleeing your residence, on Christmas Eve, no less."

"While that may be, I had another motivation to return to work." She lifted her chin. "My father is ill, yet he plans to leave on an extended voyage in three days. The botanical cure we seek to prepare is for him."

Mr. Black twisted his lips and gave Ash a sideways glance, as if he weren't convinced her answer fully explained their presence at the Lister Institute at such a late hour.

But it appeared that, in his line of work as a Queen's agent, Mr. Black was accustomed to such odd comings and goings, for he let the matter drop. "You've not seen Dr. Bracken since departing your home?" he asked.

"I have not." Pulling back her shoulders, Evie shifted and prepared to rise.

But Lord Thornton slid a piece of paper across the table. "Can you enlighten us as to your connection with Dr. Wilson?" The handwriting scrawled across the page was a tangle of chemical formulas involving numerous elemental symbols.

"Of course." Evie took a deep breath. "We are—were—composing a joint monograph concerning the roles of specific metals in medieval herbal remedies. In the first modern translation, Oswald Cockayne interprets them as magical or superstitious elements. Instead, Dr. Wilson and I argue that they are key components of the formula. Copper and silver, for example, have known antimicrobial properties."

Mr. Black looked to Lord Thornton. At the gentleman's nod, Mr. Black visibly relaxed.

Ash cleared his throat. "Any chance you might enlighten us as to why you suspect Dr. Bracken is involved in his colleague's death?"

"Any reason we ought not share?" Lord Thornton asked Mr. Black.

Mr. Black lifted a shoulder. "None. Given Dr. Bracken is hauling about an emerald ring, perhaps they're best forewarned."

"He intended to propose?" Evie's jaw dropped. "Tonight?"

"A ring?" A slow burn began to build in Ash's stomach. His own offering was much more modest. His voice rose in challenge. "How can you possibly have such information?"

"Dr. Bracken and Dr. Wilson are both candidates for the Hatton Chair of Chemistry," Lord Thornton replied. "As Dr. Wilson was one of ours—"

"An agent?" Evie asked.

Lord Thornton nodded. "With a specialty in nitroglycerin."

"That's an explosive!" she exclaimed.

"It is."

Confused, Ash countered, "But Dr. Wilson was studying the effectiveness of hawthorn, a member of the rose family, for relieving symptoms of angina, chest pain." Ash was acquainted with the man from his visits to the greenhouse to collect plant material for his work.

Lord Thornton nodded. "He was comparing its efficacy to that of nitroglycerine, a known vasodilator. A convenient cover for his production of the substance for more... volatile uses. Therefore, while accidental detonation was not an impossibility, Dr. Wilson would not have recklessly transported such a large quantity of an unstable substance on his person."

Mr. Black crossed his arms. "Handled roughly— bumped, banged or shaken—as one might expect of a crowd exiting Lister Institute for the holidays, it could easily detonate."

"And someone who knew of his research," Ash added two and two, "might take advantage of that fact. You believe Dr. Bracken slipped a vial into, say, his coat pocket."

"Aether." Evie lifted a shaking hand to her mouth. "All to eliminate competition for an academic position?"

"Dr. Wilson's work had made great strides," Mr. Black grumbled. "Dr. Bracken's research, on the other hand, was a miserable failure. His extract from the oleander plant, while effective, was acutely toxic."

"Oleandrin," Lord Thornton said. "Cardiotoxic, hepatotoxic and nephrotoxic."

"Heart, liver and kidney failure," Mr. Black added as a footnote, then pulled a face. "So many dead laboratory rats."

Lord Thornton rubbed the back of his neck. "Which leads us to suspect—"

"Dr. Bracken." Ash leaned forward and tapped two fingers upon the table. "As a member of the Chemistry department, he had the means, the knowledge and the opportunity. With a vial in place, all he needed to do was wait. When that blast shook the floor, he was standing not three feet away from me. The man smiled. *Smiled!*"

"Not, alas, an admission of guilt," Lord Thornton said.

"Nor is his melodramatic performance at the crime

scene," Mr. Black said, taking up the tale. "Nonetheless, I instructed agents to shadow his movements. After a brief stop in the library, Dr. Bracken returned home. His mother was most forthcoming. She and her son are, in her own words, very close." He rolled his eyes. "Dr. Bracken changed his attire, then retrieved an heirloom ring from the safe." Mr. Black's mouth twitched as he shifted his gaze to Evie. "Mrs. Bracken is utterly convinced of your acceptance."

Evie's lip curled.

"Though he was traced to your doorstep, Miss Brown, the direction of the crank hack he hired after he left was lost in the evening traffic. It may well be that he's drowning his sorrows in a pub."

Mr. Black looked unconvinced. Ash too had his doubts.

"Be careful, Miss Brown." Lord Thornton glanced from her to Ash. "If our summation is correct, Dr. Bracken also views you as competition. One man is already in the morgue."

"Most of him," Mr. Black quipped.

Ash cringed at the dark humor.

"We don't wish to add your corpse, Mr. Lockwood," Lord Thornton said. "Or another patient to the hospital ward where the victims are no longer in full possession of their extremities."

Mr. Black stepped away from the door. "We won't keep you any longer, but take care. Dr. Bracken appears to have a ruthless streak and," his dark gaze shifted to Evie, "a strong desire to make you his wife. Should you encounter him before we are able to locate him, send word immediately."

"Of course." Rattled, Evie rose. "About our late-night entry..."

The corner of Mr. Black's mouth curved upward. "I'll ensure the guard loses that paper. This interview never happened."

CHAPTER NINE

NO NEED TO RETURN IMMEDIATELY to the library. So long as Evie managed to tidy up before dawn, no one would be the wiser. Besides, first things first. They ought to prepare the mistletoe. It needed to be crushed, then steeped for a full day.

As such, they wasted no time dashing up the stairs to the greenhouse.

"Unbelievable," Evie commented, as they stopped before its door. The interview with two Queen's agents still weighed on her mind. "To think Dr. Bracken capable of murder."

"Enough about him." Ash pressed a hand to the gel pad and waited for the galvanometer to authorize his entry. "I refuse to let thoughts of him ruin the Christmas surprise I have in store for you."

"No need to growl about it." Puzzled, Evie nudged

his arm playfully. Was there a kernel of jealousy behind his irritation? Was it wrong of her to savor such a response, if only a little? "There's only one library patron who's caught my eye."

He smiled. "And there's only one woman I wish to lead down my garden path."

Her pulse jumped, and she shoved all thoughts of the mad chemist from her mind. Thoughts of him ought not be allowed to seep into the precious few hours she and Ash could call their own. Not when they had the whole of the greenhouse—and each other—to explore.

Click. A light blinked green.

Ash gripped the iron wheel and gave it a twist. Gears turned and the thick, metal bar slid aside with only the slightest grinding protest. More value was placed upon the herbs, shrubs and trees grown to assist and support research conducted in the laboratories below than the books and journals stored in Lister Library.

Irritation flattened her lips. A simple iron key occupied space in her coat pocket beside a tin whistle. Both about equally effective in keeping an intruder from accessing Lister Library.

Not so at the Bodleian. Since 1602 when the library first opened its doors to scholars, great value had been placed upon the manuscripts within its walls, going so far as to chain the books to their shelves and deny anyone— even King Charles the First—the ability to remove a book from the premises.

Ash yanked open the door and waved her inside.

She crossed the threshold, a magical portal into a world that felt a million miles removed from the snowy winter night of London. Snowflakes touched down upon the greenhouse roof, instantly melting to trickle away in streams. Inside the glass and iron bubble, the air was humid and warm. Plants from every corner of the globe filled the space, flourishing under the careful care of devoted botanists and horticulturalists. Someone—Ash? —had suspended odd, ruffled plants, ones that glowed with a faint green bioluminescence, along a pathway that led deeper into the foliage, a sight so utterly charming and romantic that her heart gave a great thud.

Cultivated, yet wild and free. A decided contrast to the structured order of her library.

Click. The door closed behind them, sealing them inside.

"Did you..." Dazed, Evie waved a hand, speechless at the display before her. This was far more than a mere tour. Ash offered no simple seduction, but a fairytale romance in which he'd arranged for her to step into a wonderland.

Color rose high upon his cheeks as he shrugged the rope from his shoulder and tossed the iron sickle in a corner. "I rather thought I'd be bringing you here after spending the day with your family."

"It's beautiful." She tugged off her mittens, unwound his scarf and unbuttoned her coat, hanging it upon a hook among work aprons, distressed by the sudden upwelling of emotion that caught in her throat. Her heart wanted to stay right here, with Ash, in London, rather than chase after an uncertain academic career in a town far from the bustling city she loved.

Her mind... would have to be quiet. She'd listen to its reasoning later. For now, she intended to enjoy anything and everything Ash had to offer.

"We'll wash the leaves, remove any soot and grime before steeping them in distilled water." At ease in his environment, Ash shrugged off his own coat and, turning a knob to increase the rocking motion of the Lucifer lamp overhead, led her from the entryway into a small workroom containing a sink and a squat stove with a chimney pipe that zig-zagged its way upward to exit through the ceiling. He waved a hand. "Everything we need."

Various herbs, flowers and plants dangled in bunches from the rafters, drying. Filling an entire wall was a chest bearing a multitude of small drawers, the contents of each carefully labeled. Shelves were lined with bottles containing all manner of oils, fats and extracts. Scattered over the counters below was a collection of glassware and crockery. A space that was part stillroom, part laboratory.

"Yew bark and elderberries?" she asked, planning ahead.

"*Taxus baccata*, the yew bark, will be in one of those drawers." He dropped the mistletoe into a large colander and rolled up his sleeves, a sight Evie found mesmerizing. "We'll collect the elderberries later, set them to boil in lard before straining them."

Coarse hairs glinted darkly over thick, ropy forearms.

As he washed and drained the mistletoe, strong muscles flexed. Her hands ached with the need to touch—and she had every intention of doing exactly that—but not yet. The sooner the plant was set to steep, the better.

She ought to offer her help, but a low electrical current hummed along her skin, and a coil of desire twisting tight deep inside her made it impossible to tear her eyes away.

"Evie?" Her gaze jumped from his hands to his face. Though the words he spoke were calm and reasoned, his molten gaze sent her body temperature through the roof. "If you'll fill that bottle," he tipped his head, "halfway with distilled water?"

"Of course," she breathed, reaching overhead to lift down the large, stoppered bottle he'd indicated.

"Focused on other things, were you?" Ash's eyes flashed, a gentle tease as he ripped the leaves from the plant, tossing them into an overlarge granite mortar.

Heat flashed over her skin, a burn the splash of water did little to cool. Aether, this greenhouse was too warm for woolen bodices and layered petticoats. Or waistcoats and cravats, garments Ash only half-heartedly donned when forced from this rooftop workspace and into the realm of gentlemen scientists, garments he'd not bothered to wear for their excursion into the park. She unfastened a button, loosening the collar that threatened to strangle her.

Ash crushed the mistletoe beneath a large stone pestle, pausing only to let her snatch the bruised leaves from the basin to push them into the bottle. Solid muscles shifted beneath his linen shirt as he worked, ones he'd used to pull himself hand over hand up a rope and into a tree, assisted by equally solid thighs. He was stronger than most London men. A credit to a childhood spent in the countryside.

"There's a certain private tour I've been promised." When had the cage of her corset become so restrictive? "I'm wondering what the greenhouse looks like beyond those beautiful glowing plants."

"Fungi."

She blinked. "Excuse me?"

"The hanging plants? Mycelial bioluminescence produced by *Panellus stipticus*, the bitter oyster, a North American variety of the fungus responsible for legends of foxfire. When well-hydrated, it glows. Unless it's been exposed to contaminants. There's potential there, to replace the proverbial canary in the coal mine, should anyone choose to develop it. Meanwhile, it makes a lovely ornament, does it not?" He laughed. "Don't pull a face, Evie. Enjoy them for what they are. A beautiful night-time display of enzymatic activity that, as yet, defies explanation."

Laughing, she pushed the last of the mistletoe into the glass jar, slid in the stopper, and swirled the contents. "Twenty-four hours to wait." Setting it down, she reached for a clean cloth. Wetting it beneath the water, she turned, hand raised. "Lift your shirt. We don't want that wound on your back to fester."

Without hesitation or embarrassment, he obliged. "There's some rubbing alcohol on the shelf. Next to some sticking plasters."

"Impressive, the bite of such a small contraption." Clucking her tongue, she cleaned away the dried blood, then applied the disinfectant.

Ash sucked air through his teeth, hissing a curse. "Can't say I think fondly of him."

"Mmm." Certainly she didn't enjoy the damage done to Ash, but with such a creature perched upon her shoulder, the streets of London would lose a good bit of their danger. "Done." She let his shirt fall.

Ash turned, his gaze dropping to her lips. "With all tasks complete..."

"We've nothing but time." She shivered in anticipation. "And an empty greenhouse." Solitude for a young couple was a rarity, making the dark hold of an airship an attractive location. But those memories had all but faded away. It was time to make new ones. "Whatever will we do?"

His eyes glinted, but his offer was perfectly proper. Save they were all alone in a deserted building. "We could start with a picnic, but I should warn you that I have little more at hand than the fruits that hang overhead."

Would he feed her with his bare hands? Her heart danced at the thought. "It sounds perfect to me."

Threading his fingers through hers, Ash led her from the stillroom, back into the greenhouse proper, turned toward the path, but stopped. "Wait." He plucked a cluster of flowers from a nearby plant and tucked it behind her ear. "The blooms suit you."

"Do they?" She studied the planes and angles of his face, handsome even in the dim light. While he wore no more than his shirtsleeves and trousers, she was corseted, laced and buttoned from neck to ankles. It was time to balance the scales. "Not as I'm dressed, like a tight-laced librarian. A necessary costume to work within academia, but here in such warmth? It's torture." Brazen, she unhooked the remaining clasps holding her jacket in place. "Help me take it off?"

"Unfair, I suppose, that a lady must always be so restrained." The look he gave her curled her toes as he tugged the sleeve down over her wrist.

"Please. You know I'm no lady." Free of her jacket, she quickly disposed of the cincher about her waist. Then, encouraged by the heat in his gaze, she reached to her hair and plucked free a number of pins to set them upon a nearby potting table. "Merely an aviator's daughter in disguise."

"But your medieval studies, your scholarship—"

"Is very real." She thought of the letter in her pocket, and her stomach did a flip. But to mention it now would ruin their moment. Besides, she could see worry and self-doubt creeping onto Ash's face. "Same as yours. A gardener's son rising through the ranks, first acquiring a degree in botany, and now well on his way to running an entire wing of the nation's most prestigious greenhouse."

She shook loose her long, honey-blonde hair, then closed the space between them to poke a finger into his chest. "Should education and research be restricted only to those born to the gentry? No. We earned our places here at Lister, same as everyone else who walks its halls. You button on a waistcoat and tie on a cravat to visit the library. Why? Because observing the trappings of society merely smooths the path. It doesn't change who we are. Speaking of paths..." Backing up, she held out a hand.

His eyes flashed, dark and full of delightful promises. "You do seem particularly keen on reaching its end."

She laughed, and he caught her hand in his.

Thus linked, they turned onto a flagstone path illuminated by faint moonlight and edged with the soft glow of foxfire. Step by step, reality fell away as the world of fairy encircled them. In the strange twilight, ferns brushed at her skirts and vines twisted over branches that seemed to spread their arms in welcome, some dangling strange and tempting fruits of the sort that stories and poems warned a young woman against.

The path took a turn, but at its bend was an arbor with arching latticework. A profusion of plant tendrils twined up and over and about its sheltering arch. An iron bench tucked deep in its shadows beckoned. Beneath her feet was a bed of moss, soft and yielding.

"At any moment," Evie breathed, turning about, taking in the fairyland that enveloped them, "tiny winged creatures might appear to dance by the foxfire while goblin merchants hold out their fantastic fruits in temptation."

Only one forbidden fruit interested her.

Ash reached into the foliage and plucked an oval fruit from a potted tree. He tugged her down onto the bench beside him and drew a penknife from his pocket to peel away its skin. "We've no pixies here, and you've not locks of gold to pay their price, but I can offer you nectar and sweetness from faraway lands."

"What is it?" She eyed the unfamiliar, orange fruit.

"Mango." Slicing off a section, he held it to her lips. "From India."

She opened her mouth, and he slid the juicy, sweet fruit onto her tongue. Closing her eyes, she bit down into its soft flesh. "Mmm," she hummed, sucking on his fingers. "So sweet and different, yet wonderful. I've never tasted its like."

She parted her lips, inviting more.

THE WET HEAT of Evie's mouth, the pull of her lips upon his fingers was fast burning away rational thought.

Who led who down the garden path?

He'd meant to court her first, to speak with her father, to offer a ring, *then* to bring her here to celebrate. But everything was happening in reverse. The ring burned in his pocket but, like corsets and cravats, it was merely a

societal convention. Did it really matter if they anticipated a few steps?

There would be time for a proposal.

Later.

Mesmerized, he offered Evie another slice of the ripe
mango, watching as her tongue darted out across her lips,
lapping up the escaping juices. Missing an errant trickle.
He thought to wipe it away, but stopped himself. Instead,
he licked the juice from the edge of her chin.

When her breath hitched, there was no more denying
himself, no more reining in of desire. The outside world
ceased to exist. His consciousness narrowed its focus,
centering only on the woman before him. He angled his
head and captured her soft, lush mouth. Her hands fell
upon his shoulders, fingers digging into his muscles, a
silent message that this time she had no intention of
letting him stop with a kiss.

Neither did he.

With the tip of his tongue, he traced the seam of her
mouth, teasing, coaxing. No need to press for entry, for
her lips parted and matched each stroke of his tongue
with one of her own, eager—until she shoved him away.

"Evie?" Pained, he caught her gaze. Had he misinter-
preted her eagerness? "I'm sorry, I didn't mean to—"

"No. It's not that." She pressed a finger to his mouth.
"It's simply not fair," she complained, breathless. "You,
with your scant few layers. Me, with too many to count."
Her fingers landed upon the tiny pearl buttons of her

high-necked blouse. Perfect attire for a winter's night. Not so a visit to tropics. "I want to feel the warm air on my skin." Her dark eyes captured his, and her mouth curved in the most alluring way. "*You* on my skin. *All of it.*"

Arousal tightened its grip, threatening to snap his overtaxed self-discipline. "You're certain, Evie? All we have is a bed of moss."

He wanted this so much, but neither would he push her for more than she was willing to give.

Her fingers paused at her waist and the look she gave him made his body throb with need. "If you don't think you can manage it..."

"Sprite." He laughed. "You turn my world upside-down." He ought to say no, steer her back up the path, and deliver her safely home. But he wouldn't. Not when he'd spent far too many nights imaging her here, naked and free beneath an awning of greenery. *His* greenery.

"Is that a yes?"

As if he would say no.

Grinning at her boldness, Ash tossed aside the remains of the mango, folded the pen knife, and wiped his fingers on a handkerchief. "Allow me to assist."

Buttons freed, Evie tugged the blouse off and laid it atop a shrub—then slipped her corset cover free. "That's better." Her arms, now bare, framed lovely breasts that swelled above the edge of a pale green corset. Breasts that were restrained only by a gossamer-thin cotton chemise edged in delicate lace.

His fingers itched to touch.

She leaned forward, smiling, guessing—correctly—at the thoughts running through his head.

So instead, he bent and grabbed her booted ankles, tossing up the froth of her skirts and petticoats as he swung her feet onto his lap, suddenly keen to throw her off balance. "No forest nymph wears shoes. Or stockings."

She caught at the bench, laughing. "Is that so?"

"It's a known fact." He tugged at the laces, loosening the leather that encased her feet. One boot hit the ground. The second soon followed. Beneath his palms lay nothing but thin, fine silk.

He shaped his hands to the delicate arch of her foot, wrapped thumb and forefinger about her trim ankle, then smoothed his hand over the flare of her calf. Ever upward until the pads of his fingers discovered a garter, the edge of her stocking, and—his groin tightened—the soft skin of her inner thigh.

He traced a circle, spiraled it yet higher, then lifted his gaze to hers.

Eyes dark with desire, her breath came in gentle pants and her fingers clutched at scrolls of ironwork. "Don't stop now."

Sliding on a mischievous grin, he hooked his finger over the edge of her stocking, then skimmed the silk down her leg to toss it aside.

"Ash." A faint groan of frustration hung on her exhalation.

An evil corner of his mind grinned, pleased to leave her balanced on the knife's edge of arousal, far from satisfied.

Kissing his way upward and over the remaining silk stocking, he nipped at the skin beneath, eliciting soft cries and gasps. Until his lips met soft, pliant flesh. Until he could smell her desire.

She squirmed on the iron bench.

With a quick nip, he stripped away the remaining stocking.

"Tease." The word escaped Evie's lips on a huff as she scrambled onto her feet. Deft fingers unhooked skirts, petticoats and the tie that fastened her bustle. She shoved them down over her hips and stepped free, bare feet onto stones padded by the litter of fallen leaves.

And yet there was still so very little of her he could *see*. He wanted her stripped bare. "I've yet to see a corseted nymph."

"And have you seen many?" Her eyebrows lifted.

"Corsets?" There'd been a few women, but none who'd ever occupied his every waking thought. "None since my gaze first fell upon you."

She gave him an impish smile. "And you have the only cravat to catch my eye in years. But I *meant* fairies."

"Ah. London's rather short on them." He leaned back as he pretended to pass judgment on her eligibility to dance among the fairies, his posture belying a growing hunger. "But those I have seen in the countryside have favored delicate and translucent fabrics. Or leaves."

She laughed. "If that's a hint, you'll need to loosen my laces."

Pulling aside the soft waves of hair that fell to her waist, Evie dropped onto his lap and nudged her rump against his straining erection. She wriggled, and what little blood remained in his brain drained to his lap.

"Death by slow torture," he hissed. "Channeling an imp, are we?" With thick and clumsy fingers, he fumbled with the knot at her waist. Somehow the cumbersome corset fell loose and unhooked. It—and her chemise—joined her other garments in the bushes.

She sighed. "Much better."

"Aether, you're gorgeous," he whispered. Evie, bare to the waist. His fantasies could not begin to compare.

A moment later, she straddled his lap. Then her hands were in his hair, pulling his mouth to hers, fusing their lips. Her kisses were deep and drugging, and he felt the world about him tilt and shift with each flick of her tongue against his own.

Her fingers clawed at the buttons of his shirt, flicking them free, one after the other, pushing the edges apart so that she might run her palms over the planes of his chest, his shoulders, stoking a growing fire that threatened to consume them both. From the back of her throat came a pleased hum. Never had he been so grateful for all his hard work in the greenhouse.

One hand explored the sweet curve of her backside, another cupped the weight of her breast. All while enduring the sweet torture of her squirms and wiggles against his straining erection. He rolled a single, tight nipple between thumb and forefinger, and a cry of carnal pleasure tore from her throat.

Needy, her hips flexed and his cock throbbed in response, desperate to be inside her soft, wet warmth. He grabbed at her hips and thrust upward, cursing at the layers of fabric still separating them. Enough. They had to go. "I need you, Evie. Need to be inside."

Her drawers were slitted. His trousers simply fastened. With the flick of a few buttons, he could free his erection. If the dark of her wide pupils was any indication, she might welcome a fast, rough coupling right here on the bench.

He released her hips, grasped the fastening of his waistband and—

"Not yet," she said. Her breaths came in gasps as she slid from his lap, depriving his length of the pressure it so desperately demanded. "Do you have a..."

"Sheath?" Blood at the boiling point, he had to choke out the word. "I do."

She tugged at the drawstring of her drawers, then pushed the garment over her hips. "Bring it with you, then, when you're ready to play satyr to my nymph." Snow and cloud-filtered moonlight glinted on her bare skin as she stepped off the path and disappeared into the foliage.

Without a moment's hesitation, he leapt onto his feet and yanked off his clothing, digging deep into a pocket.

All while thanking the primitive part of his brain that had insisted Evie, unleashed, possessed a wild side.

For once, the higher centers of his mind rejoiced at the stern correction.

CHAPTER TEN

F OR THE FIRST TIME IN HER MEMORY, no shoes, no stockings stood between her and the ground. Such a strange sensation to feel moss, cool and spongy, beneath her feet. No breeze stirred the moist and heavy air that hung against her skin. And—for all its tropical plants—no sounds save that of her own breaths and a frantic rustle as Ash hurried to join her.

Overhead, snowflakes alighted on the dark glass, each melting in turn to form tiny rivulets that grew into steady streams. Here, half-hidden by a screen of branches and leaves, was a secluded pocket of the greenhouse where a nymph might take a lover.

A smile stole across her face and a shiver of anticipation rippled across her skin. This was madness, yet she wanted no cure. In Ash's presence, beneath his touch, the prim and proper librarian was forgotten. Here, amidst the warmth and greenery he tended, she felt free.

Leaves rustled and Ash stepped onto the bed of moss, dropping a paper packet onto the ground beside their feet. She dragged her gaze upward, taking in every attractive inch. From the tips of his toes to the golden highlights that streaked through his hair.

A lifetime spent in the company of plants had shaped his form in the most pleasing manner. Muscular and powerful, yet capable of nurturing the most delicate of flowers.

There was no mystery as to why all flourished within his sphere.

He reached for her, drawing her close. "So beautiful," he whispered. "My heart aches."

His heart? It worried her, this growing awareness that they both wanted more beyond a fleeting affair. But Oxford's siren call could not be ignored. She'd tell him. Soon. After.

Evie shifted closer. "Oh?" She dragged a fingertip along the narrow line of hair that trailed between the ridges and planes of his stomach. Each inch brought her ever closer to his most impressive erection. "It rather appears something *else* might ache."

She wrapped her fingers around him, and the groan that escaped his lips gratified something deep and primitive inside her.

Yes.

Inside her.

That was *exactly* where he belonged.

"Imp." His hands cupped the base of her skull and

brought her mouth to his. This time there was no gentleness, no teasing. The roughness of his close-cropped beard scraped across her skin a moment before his tongue thrust into her mouth, stoking the fire inside her—inside them both—back to a fever pitch.

There was so much of him to explore. Releasing his thick member, she slid her arms around his waist and let her hands roam over his back, over the broad expanse of muscles that rippled and shifted beneath his skin with every movement. Bump by bump, she skimmed her hands downward over his spine. To the small of his back. To the swell of his buttocks.

She clutched those two mounds and pulled. His erection pressed hot and heavy against her lower abdomen. So much for her plan of patient exploration.

He broke the kiss, his beard rasping against her jawline as he whispered in her ear. "We've all night, Evie."

Lie.

Though her name on his lips was a plea for mercy, his breathlessness requested otherwise.

"Let's not pretend, shall we." She let the tips of her breasts brush across the scattering of hairs on his chest, tempting his control and heightening her own need. "Neither of us wishes to wait a moment longer. And there's always next time."

Not for a minute would she let herself believe that her professional goals would alter his personal opinion of her. No reason existed that they might not enjoy an extended affair that spanned both time *and* distance.

"Then come, my fairy queen. Fulfill a fantasy?" He caught her hand and lowered himself to the bed of moss, dragging her down with him. Atop him. "I've imagined this moment a thousand times."

Rough and heated kisses fell on the corner of her lips, the edge of her jaw, the curve of her neck. The hard planes of his chest crushed against her breasts. All wondrous, but none more so than the stiff rod pressed to her pelvis.

"The fantasy?" she whispered, roused by the notion that she'd featured in his daydreams. She was keen to learn exactly how. "For in this leafy realm you've cultivated, I've an inclination to grant a wish."

Dark eyes stared up at her. "A fair-haired fae with an inclination to ride." His fingers gripped her thighs, spreading her open above him. "Fast and hard."

A thrill rose within her. "Granted."

Pushing against solid shoulders, she levered herself upright. Dropping her knees to the moss on either side of his hips, she seated herself on his stiff length. So good, yet not nearly enough. She flexed her pelvis, dragging the wetness of her core over his thick erection. Warm currents sparked, surged outward in a thrilling rush.

Ash massaged her breasts, flicked and teased her nipples, spiraling every sensation higher.

"With the flowers in your flowing hair, and the moonlight falling upon your glowing skin," he half-whispered, half-groaned, "I almost expect you to sprout translucent and glimmering wings. Evie, I've wanted you for so very long."

"And now you'll have me." She repeated the movement, and more nerves joined in to hum their approval. A few strokes more had them both panting, and the hollow ache inside her cried out for more. It was time to ride.

Evie reached for the paper packet and pressed it into his hand. "Cover yourself."

Paper tore and Ash rolled the thin sheath over himself.

She reached for his erection.

Straddling him, she nudged the broad head of his cock against her opening, then sank onto him, inch by inch, rocking her hips, replacing the desperate ache with a full, satisfying stretch.

"So good," he murmured. "So perfect." His work-roughened palms fell at her hips, a delight against her skin. As was the awe and agony and pleasure upon his face. "Evie."

At last, her hips fell flush with his.

Full.

She fought the urge to move. Leaning forward, dropping onto her hands and letting the curtain of her hair frame their faces, she kissed Ash's lips, long and slow and deep. Then, pulling away, she gave the slightest twitch of her hips.

He groaned, then nudged upward. "More, my queen."

She rose, then sank back down, reveling in the sensations that flooded her.

"Again." Ash dug his fingers into her hips and thrust upward. The force of his grip sent a new kind of thrill through her. One that made explicit demands and dark promises.

This was, after all, the land of fairy. Neither in this world nor fully in another.

Evie threw her head backward and gave herself wholly to the experience.

She rose, then dropped her hips onto his, pushing him deep inside. Again and again. Harder. Faster. Chasing the need that shifted and grew ever deeper inside her. With each plunge, she ground her core against his pubic bone.

Small noises gathered in the back of her throat, then began to escape—one by one—each growing louder.

"Yes." His hips lifted to meet hers on the descent, plunging deeper than she'd thought possible, all while a growing pressure circled, tightening, but hovering just out of reach in the mist. Faster and harder now, her hips dropped, aided by gravity and Ash's tight grip. "Like that. Aether, yes."

"Ash... I..." Pleasure remained a mere hair's breadth away.

His hand slipped between them, pressing on that knot of nerves he'd tormented earlier. "Now, Evie," he ordered, surging into her.

Her world exploded. "Ash!" Waves of pleasure

pulsed as her sex clamped down on his shaft and sent a burst of electricity racing through her body all the way to her toes. Orgasm flooded her with heat—and love.

His hands were on her hips again, desperate in their tight grip. Lifting, pulling, he thrust deep and hard. Once. Twice. A third time he drove into her, shouting his own release.

She collapsed, melting onto his heaving chest, pressing a kiss to the hollow of his neck, before dropping her head. "That was amazing," she whispered, her breath drifting across his shoulder. "It's no wonder the nymphs cavort with satyrs, or fairy queens with masterful gardeners."

A laugh rumbled in his chest. "I should have lured you into the greenhouse months ago." A few long moments later, he rolled, lowering Evie onto the soft bed of moss before pulling free and discarding the sheath.

She wrapped her softness around his warm, hard frame and smiled against his skin. "Were the small offerings not the beginnings of a long seduction? A sweet lemon. A sprig of ivy. A tiny fir tree."

Overhead, snow now accumulated on the cold glass. On the surface of the bubble that cocooned them in a fairyland. She stroked her fingers over the hairs scattered across Ash's chest and wondered at how her world had turned upside-down and backward.

"Exactly so." His arm tightened about her waist. "How else to lure a woman such as yourself to step outside her domain and into my arms?"

Ah, yes. The other world in which she lived her life. Memories of it began to intrude. Her application for a scholarship. Work upon her monograph. Long hours in the library with Ash, working side by side as a joint project and growing flirtations led them inexorably to this, a closeness she'd never dared dream possible.

One threatened by the discovery that the dream she'd thought beyond her reach now dangled before her, a tempting fruit that would take her away from London.

Away from Ash.

She twisted in his arms. The sharp edges of tiny stones buried within the moss began to bite into her flesh, and she shifted.

"Cold?" he asked.

"Not at all." She skimmed her palm over of the flat of his stomach, willing her mind to quiet, to enjoy the moment.

It refused.

"Stay here a moment," Ash murmured, rising and taking with him his comforting warmth.

"Oh?" She threw him a seductive smile as he rose, trying hard to regain the magic that had shimmered in the air mere moments ago. "Again?"

"Not yet, sprite." A grin split his face as he pushed his way through the foliage.

She shivered at the loss of his heat. Half-reclining, Evie brushed her hand over the surface of the moss, miserable. Decisions that threatened to tear her in half needed to be made. Should she stay in London? Leave for Oxford?

Uncertainty plagued her.

Risks surrounded both decisions. Stay and chance a broken heart? What if their joint project was rejected by the committee? But after a year at Oxford, what—if anything—would be left for her in London?

Through the leaves, she could see Ash hunting through his pocket. He straightened and she caught a flash of gold.

Thunderclouds!

She bolted upright, leapt to her feet and followed him. He couldn't possibly mean to—

WITHOUT A DOUBT, Evie was the woman he wanted by his side. As his wife.

Smart. Talented. Driven. And, under the right circumstances, a little bit wild. Much like the vines he spent time cultivating. One was never certain exactly how or where they might extend their tendrils.

A thought which planted a small seed of doubt in his mind. They would make an excellent team. Both here at Lister. At home. In the bedroom where they could embark on other explorations upon a softer surface not studded with bits of gravel, sticks and dried leaves.

But would she agree?

Digging into his pocket, he pulled forth a small treasure. Between his fingers, the dull gold band glowed in the faint mycelial bioluminescent light. Across its surface, vines twisted and a flower bloomed. Though not an emerald, it was a piece of history. Locating it had involved scouring much of London, for only an original would do.

Leaves rustled, and he turned.

Evie stood upon the path, framed by rampant foliage. Her long hair cascaded in a wild tumble over her shoulders, curving about her generous breasts, its half-curled ends dancing about her navel. A magnificent sight, except her gaze was fixed upon the bauble he held, her hand upon her chest, where it traced an unsteady circle upon her breastbone. Worry churned in his stomach, but hesitation would win him nothing.

"Will you wear my ring?" He held out the ring, making the offer without dropping onto one knee. A mistake? For a tiny furrow carved itself into her forehead.

Mouth agape, she struggled to pull air into her lungs. "Ash. I—" Her hand trembled as she took it from his fingers. "*You have my hart*," she breathed, reading the inscription, with its medieval spelling, aloud. "A posey ring. Medieval. Fifteenth century."

"I thought you might like to own a piece of the past you've spent so many years studying."

"It's beautiful. The sentiment so very touching." A tremulous smile climbed onto her lips. "Where on earth did you find such a treasure?"

"In the dark recesses of a jeweler's collection. When

he realized I meant to propose, the man attempted to steer me toward something with more sparkle and shine, convinced I chose poorly." The words poured from his mouth in a long ramble. Ash studied her eyes, concerned. She'd not slipped it on her finger. "Did I? Will you wear it? Promise me you are mine and I am yours?"

A tear ran down her cheek. "I can't." She pressed the gold band back into his hand. "I don't know if I'm staying in London."

Too shocked to respond, his fingers closed around it. Without a convenient pocket, he slipped it onto the tip of his little finger for safekeeping. "But what of our plans to compile a list of medicinal plants? To see them grown? Studied in Lister Laboratories here in the city?" He swallowed, forcing back the acid that crept into his throat. "Together?"

"I know." She turned away, snatching up her chemise and drawers, avoiding his eyes. "And I will help you for as long as I'm able. Perhaps we can continue to work via correspondence."

He struggled to process the tangled knot his words had tied in their evening. Not one hour past, she'd uttered the words "next time". Had she only ever intended to take him as her lover? Did his desire for a permanent commitment scare her? Or was it something else?

Worry coalesced into dread, rising into the back of his throat, where the bitter lump proved impossible to swallow. "What has changed in the space of a few hours?"

"Chance? Fate? Luck?" Evie dropped onto the bench, yanking on her stockings and boots. The wild tumble of her hair hid her face from him. "Regardless, they all have a dreadful sense of timing."

"Luck?" Where the ground had been firm, Ash found a swampy morass. He was sinking—and fast. Like a man about to go under, he cast about for a vine that could swing him safely back to terra firma.

"When I returned home this evening," Evie said. A hint of regret threaded through her voice. "I found a letter waiting. One I never thought to receive. The Department of Medieval Studies at Oxford has offered me the position of visiting scholar, one that begins Hilary Term."

He was unaware she'd applied for such an opportunity. They'd shared so much, and yet it appeared they did not know each other as well as he'd thought. His heart shrank. "That's only a few weeks away."

"So it is." She snatched up her corset and wrapped it about her waist, fastening its hooks. "Unlimited access to the medieval manuscripts of the Bodleian Library." Her shoulders stiffened. "How can I turn down such a rare opportunity?"

How indeed? It burned to discover his status. Below books. Below Lister. Below her father. Landing him somewhere above Bracken. Such a rank failed to mitigate a rising aggravation.

"You knew this was a possibility and said nothing?" A sharp edge honed his voice, as an irritable heat coursed through his veins. He found it impossible to concede he'd lost to a pile of dusty books. "While I planned for a future, for a wife, for a union recognized by all of society, all you wanted was a lover?" Lips flattened, he snatched up his trousers and pulled them on. His fault for not keeping to the carefully proscribed steps dictated by society for a proper courtship.

"Why is it so very wrong for a woman to take a lover, when men do so with regularity?" Before him, she'd transformed into a vengeful fairy queen with cold and distant eyes. Evie hauled on her petticoats and skirts, fingers flying over the hooks and ties. "You knew I was no innocent."

"Of course." His temper snapped. "An aviator's daughter. And I'm nothing but an overreaching gardener with dirt under his nails." Ash yanked on his shirt with such violence, he all but tore the seams. Then, pulling the posey ring from his little finger, he flicked it away.

Ping!

Evie's wide eyes followed its golden arc. Her jaw dropped open, perhaps to protest, but she snapped it shut, lips pressed into a firm line.

The ring's landing went unmarked, its resting place softened by leaves or moss, he knew not. A tribute to a moment seared into his mind, one never to be repeated.

Not that he was done speaking his mind. "You presumed this would be a simple tryst? A single night of revelry? A bit of convenient fun before you left London to prowl the finer hunting grounds of Oxford?" He crossed his arms and narrowed his eyes, shocking even himself with the words that burst from his mouth. "If Bracken was a peer, a true gentleman, would you have overlooked his grasping manner and drawn him into your arms instead?"

"How dare you!" Her nostrils flared. Heat stained her face.

Good. Now they were of equal temper. Let fury reveal her true intentions. He'd know where he stood before this encounter was over. He narrowed his eyes. "How dare I what?"

"Cheapen what we've shared." She shoved the tiny buttons of her blouse through uncooperative eyelets. Body tense, she snatched up her bustle, glaring at the contraption in frustration before crumpling its wires and stuffing them beneath her arm. "The position is for *one year*. I've hope Mr. Davies will agree to arrange for a leave of absence so that I might return. Though likely he will offer no guarantees." Her eyes threw daggers. "To think I almost tossed away the chance to advance my career by remaining at the Lister Institute." She lifted her chin. "For you."

"Well, I wouldn't want to stand in the way of a *career*-minded woman." Served him right for setting his sights upon a college-educated woman. No, that was pain and embarrassment and loss putting angry words in his mouth. Her academic interests were part of what drew him to her.

Damp gathered in her eyes. A single tear slipped free,

glistening as it slid down over her cheek. He almost reached out to brush it away.

Almost.

"And so you shall not." She snatched up a fistful of her skirts. "I will inform Mr. Davies that you will require another librarian's assistance."

He'd overstepped, torched any chance that he'd had to win her hand and keep her at his side. The corners of his mouth turned down. Regret surged through him, but pride made him choke on an apology. "Evie—"

"Don't." Her eyes flashed. "You've said more than enough." She pulled back her shoulders and stomped off.

Ash stood there. *Aether, what had he done?* He *wanted* a career-minded woman. Someone who would challenge his mind and enrich his life as she pursued her own interests. A tendril of unease twisted in his gut. What he didn't want was a woman who leveraged her body or mind to climb into the ranks of society.

Like Mary.

Was it possible he'd allowed the past to decide his future?

Long moments passed while he rubbed the back of his neck. He imagined her shrugging on her coat, hefting the large glass bottle of steeping mistletoe into her arms, then—*clang*—exiting his greenhouse.

His mind rushed backward, thinking of all the hours she'd stolen from her own scholarship to devote to their joint project, to hunt for a cure for her father's tumor. That *he* might advance his career. That *her father* might be saved. With no assurance of any personal reward for all her work. Why, then, would he seek to prevent her from pursuing her own dream when an opportunity to study at Oxford presented itself?

The full weight of what he'd done dropped upon him like a felled tree. He'd snapped the fragile new shoot of their relationship. Could it be saved?

He groaned.

Steam trains ran both ways between Oxford and London. It was one term. Perhaps two. Not a permanent faculty position. Though he could not discount the possibility that they might make her such an offer.

The possibility that she might return to London, to the Lister Institute, existed, for her invaluable knowledge and insight would be made only more so after time at such an esteemed university. Especially if the library—or even the committee—was convinced of her value and elected to keep her position available.

If that was what she wanted, he would move mountains to see it done.

But, first, he needed to grovel, to beg her forgiveness.

Ash shoved his way into the greenery, dropping onto his knees to hunt for gold.

CHAPTER ELEVEN

F*INISH THE TASK.*

Mortified, Evie forced her feet to move. One step, then the next. Repeat.

The chill that gripped her chest and throat made deep, steadying breaths impossible. Heartbreak, however, would not stop her from accomplishing tonight's aim.

The pain of Ash's words would fade. Her life would move on. And, bells and blazes, she was determined Papa would still be a part of it, no matter where he floated.

She would take the details of this particular cure—along with the mistletoe—to a nearby pharmacist. Mrs. Greene would sigh, but she'd compounded a number of Evie's strange, old-fashioned formulas before. If for an exorbitant fee.

Papa would not leave London before she wheedled him into surrendering to yet one more treatment.

Exhaustion flitted about the edges of her vision. It was late, and it had been a long, trying day. Sleep would mend much of her misery, and a day spent with her family should set the rest to rights. But before she could return home to lick her wounds, she needed to put the library to rights.

Carefully, she placed the jar of steeping mistletoe upon the floor beside the library's great carved door. Her bent and crushed bustle clattered to the ground beside it. Brushing away the tears that kept escaping from her eyes and blurring her vision, she reached into her coat pocket for the iron key, only to have her fingers encounter the tin whistle the gypsy man had tossed to her.

The night had held such promise. Then, in the space of moments, it had disintegrated about her. An illusion without substance.

A lump in her throat threatened to choke her. She swallowed, hard, and squared her shoulders.

Ash could keep the useless mechanical squirrel. She hoped those red, beady eyes would stare at him in knowing accusation. A constant reminder of the night he'd undertaken to aid and awe a woman. Of the night he'd failed. Utterly and miserably.

Except he hadn't. Not until he'd accused her of conducting a meaningless dalliance while planning to husband hunt high among society's ranks.

Suspicion and mistrust had no place in any relationship. She huffed. Enough. Evie had no interest in shoring up a man's self-worth.

Except.

She dropped her forehead against the solid library door and let tears trickle down over her cheeks. One by one they dropped to the floor. Her mental tirade wasn't fair to Ash. She'd seen the pain and desolation on his face when she announced her intentions, and his resultant anger wasn't entirely unjustified. All evening she'd known of Oxford's offer, kept it hidden from him despite a nagging conscience and the certain knowledge that he'd wanted more than a short affair. Moreover, she knew of the blow a certain vicar's daughter had once dealt to his heart, and Evie had made no effort to challenge his assumption that she might hold similar goals.

Ash was not the only one in the wrong. She too bore a certain responsibility for the disaster that the evening had become.

Ought she turn around, climb the stairs, lay bare her emotions, and see if they might repair the rift between them?

Yes.

But the hour grew late.

Or was it early?

Regardless, those books *must* be returned to their crates. How many had they emptied? Two? If she hurried, the task would not take long.

Fishing the iron key from her coat pocket, she jammed it into the keyhole. Twisted.

Click.

She gave the heavy door a shove. About to lift the precious mistletoe tonic, she froze. *Hell's bells.*

Across the room, the fire snapped and crackled in the grate. Before it, Dr. Bracken reclined in a wingback chair twisting that horrid mustache about his finger. Beside him, *Hardwicke's Leechbook* rested upon the table alongside the china teapot and cups. Most concerning, however, was the notebook propped upon his lap. It contained the entirety of the project she and Ash intended to present before the review committee.

With great attentiveness, Dr. Bracken perused its contents.

The sharp claws of a pteryform sank deep into her chest and squeezed.

"Do come in, Miss Brown," he called, setting aside the notebook and rising. As if nothing were amiss. As if he'd not broken into the library. Not manufactured an explosive chemical to ensure the incendiary death of a competitive colleague. "We've much to discuss."

Take tea with a murderer? Not a chance.

Stepping backward, she gathered up the length of her skirts, readying herself to run. Ought she dash down the stairs in the hopes that Mr. Black and Lord Thornton still lurked about the morgue? Or race for the door and take her chances in the streets?

"I'd rather not give chase, Miss Brown." Dr. Bracken lifted the ancient manuscript and held it over leaping flames.

Heart in her throat, she froze. "You wouldn't."

"Oh, but I would." There was no hesitation, no tension in his shoulders, no indication at all that he might be bluffing. "Given the hour, the date, and the reverence with which this text was laid out upon the table beside a most fascinating notebook, I gather you intend to further your career by incorporating the contents of this tome into this project you've formulated. Run, and I'll destroy what must be a groundbreaking treatise on medieval medicine." The hard edge of his voice bit to the bone.

"Don't." She was a fool. Bargaining for a book with a man willing to snuff out a life on Christmas Eve. Against her better judgment, Evie stepped inside the library and shoved the heavy, oak door closed with her backside, praying that security might notice the unusual flask of liquid and a woman's bustle in the hallway and seek to investigate. Odds were, however, low.

Insides aquiver, she crossed the room.

Dr. Bracken replaced the manuscript, then assisted her with the removal of her old wool coat. As she perched upon the edge of the wingback chair, his gaze traveled over her disheveled form. Frowning, he tsked. "How very disappointing to find a grain of truth in the public's perception. An airship captain's daughter who, despite years of education and training, stoops low to rut with a gardener. One who, it seems," he plucked a leaf from her tousled hair that she'd not yet pinned back into place, "could not be bothered to so much as spread a rough blanket upon the ground. I'd thought better of you."

Indignant, Evie wanted to scream in protest, but—

though her face burned—she'd not dignify his comments with a response. "If you'd wished to discuss my research project, you only needed to ask." A lie, but one must appease such a man. "It's a fledgling idea, one that would no doubt benefit from your expertise and insight."

"That's better." He lowered himself into the chair across from her, perfectly at ease. Madness personified, yet every inch the gentleman, from his pressed trousers to his starched collar. A diamond pin winked from the deep folds of his silk cravat, neatly tucked beneath his double-breasted, brocade waistcoat. He tapped the cover of the notebook. "The data you've gathered here is enough to keep several scientists occupied for years."

Unfortunately, it was also neatly penned and outlined. She'd all but tied it up with a bow.

Her skin prickled. "It is."

"Do endeavor to explain why you've kept this bit of brilliance tucked away." Dr. Bracken leaned forward. His eyebrows lifted and drew together, furrowing his brow. "When you well-knew I was looking to find exactly such a project."

Heat gathered beneath her collar, all but choking her. She forced her eyes wide when all she wished to do was narrow them and spit at him in anger. "I directed your attention to ginger, did I not? It is a most promising plant."

Disappointment twisted his lips. Did he expect her to pander to his ego and grovel? Most probably.

"My dear, you are not a trained scientist, merely a

librarian. It is not your place—or a gardener's—to judge which project might best suit my needs. You offered me a tiny dribble of information, when what you should have offered me was full and unrestricted access." He snatched up the notebook and leaned backward, crossing a leg as he flipped through a few pages. "Here, the data is collated and cross-referenced, not merely suggesting the individual constituents of a single plant. Progress has been made correlating various recipes—including details of their preparations—with a variety of illnesses. A project of considerable complexity with the potential to transform the practice of medicine, tossing aside the nonsense of medieval magical beliefs to extract the active ingredients."

To think Ash had accused her of trawling for a peer. What use had she of men who expected the world to serve them? Lazy was one of Dr. Bracken's defining personality traits, though he was perfectly capable of innovative thought. He was bright, well-educated, and had access to resources of which most men could only dream.

Including hers.

In the few short hours she'd spent with Ash away from the library, Bracken had divined the entirety of their plans and recognized their brilliance. Her stomach knotted for—she could see it in the flare of his eyes—he intended to take it for himself, use it to advance his faltering career.

With no conclusive proof of his guilt, would the

Queen's agents be able to press charges? Might he escape all blame? Would the board of the Lister Institute grasp the long-range and broad possibilities of the medicinal plant project, and convince themselves that there were no risks, only benefits, in appointing the chemist to the Hatton Chair?

"Many of these recipes are complex, which makes them perfect for investigation. Take this eye salve, for example." Bracken read aloud from the notebook. "Onion or leek. Garlic. Wine. Ox gall. A brass vessel. Mix and let sit for nine days." He smiled, smug. "A laboratory project easily conducted. We test the antimicrobial activity of all combinations in order to tease out any and all active ingredients. Brilliant."

It was. Not that he would be claiming any of it for his own. But it would be ill-advised to rile a man prepared to eliminate the competition. She folded her hands in her lap and kept her thoughts to herself.

Dr. Bracken flipped a page, slowly shaking his head. "Mr. Lockwood is, without an advanced degree, a mere gardener. He is *not* the man to develop such a project, merely the one who should execute the commands as to which plants ought be grown. I, on the other hand, have the background for such an undertaking. As my wife—"

"Wife?" An icy dagger scraped down her spine.

Married, he would be within his rights to dictate and manage every aspect of her life. From the direction of the projects she worked upon to the conditions of their marital relations. Her skin crawled at the thought of his hands groping her bare flesh.

His features tightened. "Do endeavor to not interrupt, Miss Brown. As my wife, you *would have* been relieved of all the mundane responsibilities of a librarian." He tugged a small box from inside his coat. Flicking open its lid, he stared at the glimmering emerald and diamond ring within, mournful. "But I cannot take a bride with such appalling restraint." He snapped the box shut and tucked it away. "And you know too much."

Evie's heart pounded at the evil glint in his eye. Did he mean to do her harm? No, he couldn't possibly. Nonetheless, she hastened to humor him. "You are, of course, correct. Take the notebook. Consider it my Christmas gift to you."

"Thank you." He poured a single cup of tea with a sigh, as if the task was too burdensome. "Alas, it is too little, too late." From another pocket, he produced a small vial filled with a fine, white powder. He pulled the cork free and upended its contents into the teacup before setting it before her. "Consider my quandary. You're an unusually intelligent female. I can't let you walk free. But in the spirit of reciprocity and a nod to the holiday, I will offer you a choice as to how your corpse is found."

"My corpse?" The words wheezed from her chest.

Dr. Bracken produced a pistol. Firelight glinted off the intricate, engraved scrollwork. "A woman traipsing about the streets alone in the dark of night. A wrong turn down a dark alleyway. Who would be surprised to learn of the horrible death she suffered refusing to hand over her purse to a common criminal?"

Spots appeared in her field of vision. She gripped the edge of the table, willing the numbness in her fingers to cease. Would informing him that the Queen's agents had cause to question him help or hurt her cause? All pretense of charm had fallen away from Dr. Bracken's face. His eyes were dead and cold. Hurt, she decided. If he knew Mr. Black was in pursuit, no one would ever find her corpse.

From the corner of her eyes, she cast about, looking for something—anything—she might wield in self-defense. "You'd chance ruining your sartorial splendor with a spray of blood?"

"I would." His icy stare froze the blood in her veins. "Though hemlock is a rather slow-acting poison, it *is* painless. The better choice. They'd find your corpse here, slumped in a chair. Overcome with shame, Miss Brown took her own life. If questioned, I'll inform the Queen's agents of your flirtation with the gardener. Drop hints that he pressured you, suggest that your," his lip curled, "disheveled state implies you were forced against your will. Who won't believe that you took your life after such an assault? Either way, the project is mine."

Rape.

She would be dead, and Ash would lose his position. The repercussions he would suffer would be far, far worse than any pain her heated words had already caused him. Alternatively, she could die alone, cast into the gutter of an obscure alley. Either way, her family would be devastated. Her hands began to shake.

Was there any hope of escaping this nightmare?

A distant blur of motion caught her eye.

CHAPTER TWELVE

Finding the posey ring had taken far too long. Searching the ground had turned up nothing. Only when he'd straightened, close to abandoning hope, had he spied the glinting circlet, resting upon the broad leaf of a taro plant.

Ash had snatched it up, then stuffed his feet into his shoes and his arms into his coat. The streets of London weren't safe at this hour and, though Evie would protest, he'd see her safely home.

He would apologize. On his knees—no—prostrate on the ground before her, all while begging her forgiveness for the horrible words he'd uttered, for the irreparable harm he'd done to any future they might have shared. She would, however, be within her rights never to speak to him again.

If so, then he would take himself off to drown his sorrows in a pint of wassail, heavy on the brandy.

Chit. Chit. Chit. The lump in his pocket shifted. He pulled out the clockwork squirrel with needle-sharp claws and honed incisors, flicking its nose. Mengri stared back with those horrid red eyes, alert but inactive. Until a command was called and a note played upon the tin whistle.

He frowned. Evie could take the cursed contraption, or he'd turn it over to the Rankine Institute for analysis and dissection.

The sound of his heavy, sorry footfalls echoed in the deserted hallway. Had she already left? No. There beside the library door sat the bottle of steeping mistletoe. His heart twisted at the memory of the kiss they'd shared in Hyde Park beneath the oak tree, one full of such promise. There was little hope he'd ever find Evie's equal.

He pushed on the heavy door, grumbling about the non-existent library security. Then jerked to a halt, praising the man who had kept the hinges of the door well-oiled. Before the fire sat Bracken—with every ounce of his attention focused upon Evie.

This was why the Queen's agents had been unable to locate their suspect. Somehow, Bracken had discovered both that she was not at home, and that she meant to pass the night here, in the library. He'd invaded her sanctuary and, finding her absent, made himself comfortable while awaiting her return.

Ash knew well how much she detested the man. What could have induced her to enter the library knowing he was present? Why did she sit so still, focused upon the cup of tea Bracken poured?

A single cup.

Something was very wrong.

Dropping down onto all fours, Ash crawled into the room, pushing the door gently closed behind him. Mengri scurried upward onto his back, nails digging through the wool of his coat and into flesh as they sought purchase. Crouching behind the massive circulation desk, he caught snatches of their conversation.

Bracken intended to claim all their work—the botanical list, the cross-referenced charts, the detailed reference—for himself. Along with any credit if—no, when—biochemical studies provided insight leading to a medical breakthrough.

Insults.

A pistol.

Hemlock tea.

And an implication of sexual assault.

Shit. Aether, the man was cold.

Meanwhile, his own blood boiled.

Ruining Ash's future was nothing compared to what the man planned to do to the woman he loved. He wanted to tear the chemist limb from limb.

Ash considered his approach, clenching his teeth so hard bright spots flashed before his eyes. All he had in his possession was a small penknife. What to do?

Rush forward, fists raised?

No. With that pistol in hand, Bracken would shoot Evie long before Ash reached him.

Ought he run for the morgue to flag Mr. Black?

No. By the time they returned, it might well be too late.

Mengri.

Her coat—with its deep pocket and the gypsy's tin whistle—was within arm's reach. With one short note, the creature could be instructed to attack, subjecting Bracken to a world of chaos and pain. And handing the advantage of surprise to Ash.

Curling his lip, he pried the mechanical squirrel with its red, glowing eyes from his back. Setting the creature atop the desk, he willed the squirrel to chatter, for Evie to glance in the contraption's direction. This *had* to work. He couldn't lose her. Not like this.

"Certainly this situation need not be resolved by murder?" Evie's voice shook, making Ash grind his teeth. "This ancient book is in Old English, a language I can easily read. I can help you." She reached for *Hardwicke's Leechbook.*

"Leave it." Bracken's voice was sharp. "It's easy enough to find another translator. Drink, Miss Brown. Think of your family. It will be so much more tidy for them to find you here tomorrow morning..."

Enough. Ash rapped from the underside of the desk, attempting to rouse the contraption.

Chit. Chit. Chit.

"What was that?" There was a soft scrape, the sound of a man rising from his chair.

"Oh!" Evie exclaimed. "That?" Surprise metamorphosed into calculation as she realized Ash must be inside the library, ready to come to her aid. It soothed the ache in his heart ever so slightly.

Though they were far from safe.

"A ridiculous clockwork contraption," she said. "A curiosity purchased from a gypsy."

"It was not there a minute ago." Suspicion tinged Bracken's comment.

"On the contrary, it's been there the entire evening." A certain impishness filled Evie's voice. She'd warmed to the idea of sending the waistcoat-wearing squirrel after Bracken, and there would be no stopping her now. Did her chin lift?

There was a long silence.

"Lies are unbecoming," Bracken replied. Ash imagined his baleful stare. "Why do its eyes glow red?"

"An excellent question." Her skirts rustled. "Perhaps it helps the creature see in the dark?"

Ash needed to create a distraction, anything to present Evie with an opening to reach her coat. He knocked again on the underside of the desk, just beneath the squirrel.

"Who's there?"

The chemist wasn't stupid. He'd figure things out soon enough. Footsteps approached. Stopped.

Bracken was so close. So very close.

There was a faint *thunk* followed by a rattle. Did the chemist set down his weapon to lift the malicious clockwork squirrel, to turn it over in his hands?

Distracted, possibly disarmed, Bracken would not be prepared for an attack.

Moreover, he was nowhere near Evie.

Impossible to ignore the chance to catch the man unaware.

Snatching up a heavy tome from a cart stacked with books, Ash crept around the edge of the desk. Still crouching, he lifted the book and caught Evie's gaze.

She glanced at her coat and gave him a slow nod.

"Go!" he mouthed.

Evie reached for her coat.

"What are you doing, Miss Brown?" Bracken dropped the squirrel with a clatter, and Ash heard the scrape of a pistol being snatched up.

"I've chosen the London streets," she responded, her voice quivering.

"Really," Bracken growled, suspicious. He brandished the weapon at her. "Don't think there will be any help for you there."

Unacceptable.

Ash rose and heaved the book at Bracken, smacking him hard upon the back. *Thud.* As he ducked, Bracken spun, pointed the pistol and fired.

Bang!

Ash's heart rate spiked. The hair above his ear had

registered the bullet's trajectory as it passed. Far too close for comfort. The man's aim was surprisingly good.

Evie had used the moment to dash for the relative safety of the stacks and crouched, half-hidden behind shelves of books. Relief swept over him.

"Lockwood?" Ash could hear the sneer as it crept onto Bracken's face. "Another silly gift. I should have guessed." Bracken sighed. "It appears I shall have two bodies to dispose of instead of one. Stand up!"

And die like a man? No, thank you.

Evie lifted the tin whistle to her lips.

"Such an onerous task," Ash agreed, keeping Bracken distracted from his crouched position. "You've grown spoiled, what with the Queen's agents arriving to scrape up Dr. Wilson's remains on your behalf."

"You can prove nothing," Bracken hissed.

"Unnecessary. The Queen's agents have all they need. You won't get far," Ash warned. "Mr. Black is looking for you even now. He's spoken with your mother and is well aware of your interest in Miss Brown. Mr. Black is known for his tracking skills, and I expect him to arrive at any moment."

"I don't believe it." But his voice had lost some of its bluster.

Across the room, Evie's fingers found the top three holes. A single, clear piercing note sounded, just as the gypsy had instructed.

Bracken gave a shout. "What—"

"Mengri!" Evie yelled. "Attack!"

Screech. Chit. Chit. Chit. The clockwork squirrel scurried across the surface of the desk on needle-like nails, directing his attention at the one individual present who had not been recorded on the internally embedded cribiform wick. *Screech. Chit. Chit. Chit.*

"Meet Mengri," Ash called, relieved to relinquish the role of prey to a more worthy individual. "Miss Brown's most persistent and *sharp* guardian."

Bang! Bracken took aim at the contraption and missed. *Bang!*

Abandoning the small moving target with a curse, the chemist backed away.

Screech. Chit. Chit. Chit. Mengri leapt to the floor, chittering as he advanced upon Bracken, eyes flashing. Red. White. Red. White.

How many bullets did such a weapon hold? Five? Six?

"Attempting to hide, Miss Brown? Only natural, I suppose." Bracken pointed the weapon in her direction, keeping a close eye on Ash's position. All while Mengri stalked him, chiding as he darted behind table legs and chairs, scurrying ever closer while taking the measure of his target. "Do you think to keep me occupied with this sinister gypsy's toy? It won't work." He crossed to the table and scooped up *Hardwicke's Leechbook.* "Agents are in pursuit, are they? Then it is time to take drastic action. Sadly, it appears they won't arrive in time to preserve your discovery."

"Don't!" Pain strangled Evie's cry.

"No?" His voice mocked. "Let's examine your values." Bracken held the manuscript above the flames, threatening a treasure trove of lost knowledge. Hidden in private libraries for centuries, safely gathering dust, only to be destroyed at the hands of a raving egomaniac. "What are you willing to do to stop me, Miss Brown? Will you give your life to save a piece of history?"

Shit.

Ash had watched her caress its time-worn cover, turn its pages with awe and reverence, soaking in words of wisdom written in a dead language. Such an ancient text offered far more than a possible cure for her father. In her hands, the translation and subsequent study of such a book would garner far more than academic accolades, it promised to tease the minds of countless biologists by hinting at unknown medical remedies.

He could not—would not—let a grasping, vindictive murderer destroy it.

Gripping the sides of the library cart, Ash crouched behind it and ran forward, pushing it across the reading room. Mengri leapt aboard, screeching his displeasure as the two of them advanced upon the chemist. *Screech. Chit. Chit. Chit.*

"No answer, Miss Brown? Well then." Bracken dropped the leather-bound manuscript into the fire.

"No!" Evie yelled.

Ash prayed she would not rush forth from her hiding spot before he had a chance to—

"Stop!" Bracken yelled.

Bang!

Bits of paper and leather flew through the air above Ash's head as another bullet passed far too close. He increased his speed, running now.

Bang!

An intense, hot pain exploded across the top of his shoulder. *Shit.* He'd been hit.

At full speed, Ash slammed the cart into Bracken.

Crash!

A heartbeat later, the clockwork squirrel leapt, sinking razor-sharp incisors into the man's arm.

Bracken screamed, flinging the pistol aside, clawing at the contraption that attacked without mercy.

Evie appeared from behind the bookcase at a full sprint, diving for *Hardwicke's Leechbook,* shoving her bare hands into the flames to yank its fragile parchment pages free. With a pained cry, she dropped the book upon the marble hearth and smothered the flames with her woolen coat, beating the tome to extinguish the last of the flickering flames.

Bracken bellowed as he staggered about the room, smacking at the squirrel who refused to relinquish its grip.

Holding one hand to his shoulder to stem the flow of blood, Ash snatched up the pistol—now empty of bullets —and ran to her side at the moment she flipped back the corner of her coat.

The rare text bore scorch marks but had survived relatively unharmed.

He dropped beside her, catching her frantic hands one at a time, checking them for burns but finding nothing too serious. A tear ran down her stricken face. "Don't cry, Evie. The damage to the manuscript is minimal. And our notebook is safe."

"You came." Distress contorted her face. "I thought after our— You're bleeding!"

She pushed at his hand until he lifted it away. The wound stung something awful, but—he peered downward—the gash did not appear too deep. "Five bullets and only one managed to graze my shoulder. I'll be fine." Eventually. He glanced across the library.

Not so Bracken, who was having no success at dislodging Mengri. Rivulets of blood now streaked his once-handsome visage.

Ash turned back to Evie. "I'm sorry." He brushed away a tear. "Can you ever forgive me?"

She'd torn away a portion of her petticoat and, frowning, pressed it against the bleeding gash. "You realize I've no interest in a title, don't you? Nor any of the responsibilities or social ridiculousness that accompanies such status? I'm not Mary."

The vicar's daughter, a woman who had set her sights on climbing the social ladder by any means available to her.

"Jealousy," he drew in a deep breath, "is an ugly emotion. My words were harsh, resentful, and should never have been spoken." Would she give him a second chance?

"It was wrong, what she did." Evie's lips pressed into a thin line, but her expression softened ever so slightly. "But you can't paint all women with the same brush. I'm not her."

"I know that. I do." He kissed her soot-stained hand. "And I'm very sorry. I had such plans for Christmas Day, for us. I thought after we—" He closed his eyes for a moment. "I assumed too much, then leapt to an unwarranted conclusion."

She nodded. "Apology accepted." Her face warned him that there'd better not be a next time. "It was wrong of me not to tell you of the letter, of my plans to attend Oxford. Can you forgive me as well?"

"Of course." Did this mean he still had a chance to win her heart? His heart gave a great thud. "Dare I hope you want me to wait for you? That there's a hope your future plans might still include me?"

Screaming filled the cavernous reading room as Bracken raged, trying—and failing—to dislodge the devilish clockwork squirrel. Ash was satisfied to note he was losing the battle. With wild eyes and tangled hair, Bracken spun in drunken circles, swatting at the vicious creature as it scurried across his shoulders, sinking teeth and claws into vulnerable flesh.

"The scholarship encompasses two full terms." Evie avoided the question, pulling away. "But offers no promises of a future at Oxford. After? I've no idea what my future holds." Her face sagged. "It might be best that I decline their offer. Working at the Lister Institute is a privilege few ever win."

Hope ignited. "But you want it, those Oxford terms."

"Who wouldn't?" Another tear ran down her cheek.

"The Lister Institute would be foolish not to hold your position for you," he said. "And I don't want to be the reason you decline. But neither do I want to lose you." He drew in a deep breath. A relationship ought not require constant proximity. "Trains travel to Oxford. Both ways. Daily."

"So they do." Was that encouragement he saw in her eyes?

He took a deep breath. "I gather the offer from Oxford is to study medieval manuscripts?"

The chemist howled. "Get! It! Off!"

Clang. Crash. Clunk. The battle raged on. *Screech. Chit. Chit. Chit.*

Neither Ash nor Evie were inclined to provide aid, for the question of their new, fragile relationship held the entirety of their focus.

"It is. I plan to study the connections between modern medicine, chemistry, and its origins in alchemy." She gave him a tremulous smile and held out an olive branch. "However, as I will have no library duties to which I must attend, there's another manuscript to which I could devote a fraction of my time. Ashmole 1505. A copy of Bernard de Gordon's *Lilium medicinae* in Middle English—as yet untranslated—describing the causes and treatments of diseases such as plague, tuberculosis, and leprosy. Sections of it will contain herbal formulae that fit within the overarching goal of our proposal to the Lister Institute."

He brightened. "Are you suggesting—"

"That we continue our collaboration." Why had such a thought not already occurred to her? Because, in the time since she'd received the acceptance letter, she'd done nothing but worry about how Ash might react. With some justification.

But he'd made amends and quickly.

Why not, then, see what they might make of this growing romance?

She wanted him. She also wanted all the possibilities that her time at Oxford would offer. Greedy? She didn't care.

"As the Bodleian Library is notorious for refusing to allow a text to be removed from its halls," Evie ventured, "we could propose that my time at Oxford be used, in part, to compile a more comprehensive overview of the uses of various native plants in medicine."

"Brilliant." Ash pressed a kiss to her lips, one she returned with equal ardor. "If it's what you want, I'll do everything I can to support a leave of absence, followed by a return to your position here in the Library. No, a different position—one where you might devote more of your time to scholarly activities."

"We'll see how much latitude the board is willing to allow," Evie said, beaming. Was it possible she would be invited to return, that Ash would wait for her?

He swallowed. "I'll miss you, Evie Brown."

There was a loud crash—and yet more screaming—as Dr. Bracken overturned a cart filled with books.

Screech. Chit. Chit. Chit.

They ought to subdue the murderer. Drag him bound, hand and foot, to Mr. Black, but the rift between her and Ash was not yet fully repaired.

"Any chance we might find the posey ring?" she asked, stomach fluttering. Was she truly about to do this, to promise herself to a man?

"This, you mean?" Ash produced the gold medieval band from deep within his pocket.

"Ask me again," she prompted.

"Will you," Ash caught up her hand, "Miss Evangeline Brown, promise yourself to me and no other while we explore the possibilities of what we might build together?"

She took the ring from him, began to slide it onto her finger, but paused. "A prolonged engagement, in which we might visit each other, taking advantage of each and every unchaperoned garden path and arbor?"

His smile left her breathless. "If you insist."

"I do." She slipped the circlet onto her finger, then caught the sides of his face, dragging his mouth down to hers.

You have my hart. He did indeed.

Weapon drawn, Black kicked open the library door.

Screech. Chit. Chit. Chit.

Strewn across the ground was a confusion of books, Dr. Bracken's mewling, bleeding and prostrate form—arms wrapped about his head in self-preservation—and the blur of a familiar bristle-tailed, waistcoat-wearing, clockwork squirrel. One mounting a relentless and vicious attack upon a suspected murderer.

Across the room, a pistol lay upon the carpet beside the fire beside an upended tea table—and Miss Brown and Mr. Lockwood. A pair who, at his arrival, struggled to extricate themselves from each other's arms and rise to their feet.

Black sighed. *Lovers and villains.*

Of late, such was his lot.

To save himself trouble, he took aim, firing a single TTX dart into Dr. Bracken's sorry arse, indulging in a grim smile as his form fell limp. Then, slipping two fingers into his mouth, he gave a sharp whistle. *"Rúkker-saméngri! 'Chavaia!'"*

The mechanical rodent froze.

Black turned to the lovers. "Start explaining." He lifted a hand, eyeing Miss Brown's tousled hair and the gold band about her finger. Much, it appeared, had passed between them since their midnight interview. "Leaving out anything you do not wish recorded in my official report."

EPILOGUE

December 25, 1885

THIS YEAR, TO CELEBRATE the new beginnings signified by Evie's recent marriage, the Yule log her family had chosen was birch.

She leaned her head on Ash's shoulder and smiled, more content than she'd thought possible. Though it was cozy here before the fire, they needed to depart soon. Tomorrow, weather permitting, she and her new husband traveled north to Boroughbridge where they would spend the remainder of the year with his family.

Christmas Day had been spent with her own, but the hour now grew late.

While Beatrix and her husband struggled to settle their six young, overstimulated, over-fed children in their beds, Papa—rum in hand—expounded upon the many merits of his next voyage. A final attempt to convince them to float with him across the Atlantic. Few airships did so, as the crossing was long and not without its perils. Among the many irritants to airship captains was the requirement of a water-bound, steamer escort that would carry the necessary coal supplies to power them over the ocean.

"Are you certain you're not interested in speaking with the Mayans about their plants?" Papa lifted an eyebrow, directing his question at the newlyweds. He and Davy, still as thick as thieves, were set to pilot an airship to British Honduras. "An entire wing could be added, all aimed at growing the medicinal plants of the New World. Certainly the Lister Institute would approve such a working honeymoon? Come with me."

The past year had passed in a happy blur.

Living in Oxford and spending her days inside the Bodleian Library surrounded by ancient books had been a rare privilege she would cherish always—with Ash's frequent visits the highlight of many a weekend. Not that she'd let thoughts of him distract her. Well, not much. During the days and weeks they were apart, she'd managed to not only complete her monograph, but to compose two more.

Ash too had been productive. After the review committee had enthusiastically approved their joint project, he'd thrown himself into its oversight, gathering and planting every flower, herb, shrub or weed they'd deemed of interest—all while successfully luring scientists into the greenhouse to discuss the project's research potential.

Already, two laboratories had undertaken studies yielding promising results. And a third now studied a particular mistletoe, yew and elder solution that held a deep, personal significance.

Last Christmas, she and Ash had compounded the mistletoe, yew and elder solution discovered within *Hardwicke's Leechbook* and forced it upon her father before he floated away to Japan. It had been a stunning success.

Delivered by hypodermic needle as a subcutaneous injection over the course of nine weeks, it had effected the complete and total eradication of her father's skin lesion, a cure that had renewed Papa's exuberance for travel and brought him out of retirement.

Additionally, following the events of last December when they'd helped the Queen's agents lock away a murderer, the board was well-pleased with Evie and Ash, granting their every request.

However...

Ash tightened his arm about her shoulders. "There's little chance of convincing Mr. Davies to let your daughter float to the new world after relinquishing her talents to Oxford for months on end." He smiled at her, skimming his fingertips lightly atop the fine silk of her sleeve and sending shivers of anticipation down her spine. "He grows especially impatient for her to resume work upon the detailed translation of *Hardwicke's Leechbook*."

"Suit yourselves." Papa huffed. He was forever attempting to lure her—and now her husband—on a globe-trotting adventure despite repeated assurances that she and Ash were quite content to remain here in foggy old England. "We'll be abroad for some time. I'm of a mind to take a gander at these Mayan temples Maudslay and others are finding in the jungle."

"Well, Papa." Evie rose, kissing her father upon the cheek. Fascinating though these archeological ruins no doubt were, contemplating their exploration was not at all how she intended to spend the remainder of her evening. "It's time the newlyweds made their way home."

Goodbyes were said, cheeks kissed and hugs exchanged. Coats were collected, mittens donned, scarves wrapped and, at last, a crank hack hailed.

"Finally." Ash slipped an arm around her waist, nibbling softly at her ear as they rattled and bumped along the street. "Must we return home, my fairy queen?"

Her heart rate jumped, sending a rush of warmth through her veins. Anticipation, heightened by long glances and stolen touches, had kept her teetering on the edge of desire the entire day. Though their bed was snug, cozy and soft, other... opportunities existed tonight.

"When the Lister greenhouse is so rarely empty?" She slipped a hand along Ash's thigh, eliciting a groan. "You need to ask?"

ABOUT THE AUTHOR

Though ANNE RENWICK holds a Ph.D. in biology and greatly enjoyed tormenting the overburdened undergraduates who were her students, fiction has always been her first love. Today, she writes steampunk romance, placing a new kind of biotech in the hands of mad scientists, proper young ladies and determined villains.

Anne brings an unusual perspective to steampunk. A number of years spent locked inside the bowels of a biological research facility left her permanently altered. In her steampunk world, the Victorian fascination with all things anatomical led to a number of alarming biotechnological advances. Ones that the enemies of Britain would dearly love to possess.

www.AnneRenwick.com

instagram.com/anne_renwick
facebook.com/AnneRenwickAuthor
pinterest.com/AuthorAnneRenwick

Made in the USA
Columbia, SC
13 November 2024

c13f50fa-0a53-4559-a940-c73f6f2b82ddR03